ellipsis
• • •
press

Also by Karen An-hwei Lee

Fiction

Sonata in K (Ellipsis Press)

Translation

*Doubled Radiance: Poetry and Prose of
Li Qingzhao* (Singing Bone Press)

Poetry

What the Sea Earns for a Living (Quaci Press)

Phyla of Joy (Tupelo Press)

Ardor (Tupelo Press)

In Medias Res (Sarabande Books)

God's One Hundred Promises (Swan Scythe Press)

THE MAZE OF TRANSPARENCIES

KAREN AN-HWEI LEE

Copyright © 2019 by Karen An-hwei Lee

Portions of this book have appeared in somewhat different form in *The Collagist, Diode, The Ellis Review,* and *Moria.*

Design by Corey Frost and Eugene Lim
Cover art by Ernst Haeckel

First Edition
ISBN 978-1-940400-09-9

Ellipsis Press LLC
P.O. Box 721196
Jackson Heights, NY 11372
www.ellipsispress.com

LIBRARY OF CONGRESS CATALOGING-IN-PUBLICATION DATA

Names: Lee, Karen An-hwei, 1973- author.
Title: The maze of transparencies / Karen An-Hwei Lee.
Description: First Edition. | Jackson Heights, NY : Ellipsis Press LLC, [2019] | Includes bibliographical references.
Identifiers: LCCN 2019000367 | ISBN 9781940400099 (pbk.)
Subjects: | GSAFD: Science fiction. | Fantasy fiction.
Classification: LCC PS3612.E3435 M39 2019 | DDC 813/.6--dc23
LC record available at https://lccn.loc.gov/2019000367

A data bank holding all the information
in the universe can be found in God.
—Sunday Adelaja

The cloud is a topography
or architecture of our own desire.
—Tung-Hui Hu

Maybe stories are just data with a soul.
—Brené Brown

Shut up the words, and seal the book,
even to the time of the end: many shall run to and fro,
and knowledge shall be greatly expanded.
—Daniel 12:4, *King James Version*

THE MAZE OF TRANSPARENCIES

✦

Architecture of data, once pools of bytes
grafted to our flesh—
        cloudbanks stopped monitoring our moods. No satellites
whisper geolocations in our earbuds, no hotfix salves
                fight our affluenza—
                electromagnetic fields of viral immunity
                        fail after a fiscodigital apocalypse—
the future of collapse is here-and-now,
this age of crisis. No amanuensis
        translates us into fiber-optic light—

Nevertheless, this morning of zeroization, we wake
                with pixel-dust on our eyelashes—
only a transparent maze, dexterous web of information
moored to clouds
        blossoming
            with wingless phenomena.

CONTENTS

✦

One | The Garden Of Austerity

THE GARDEN OF AUSTERITY

Dear millennium, yours is a thinly veiled gospel of austerity
driven by forces of recession foreshadowing divestitures

and dysthymia, of blissful returns plunged into depression,
orange blossoms ignoring the self-governance of data

in yesterday's flowering courts of equilibrium and forecasts—
an analyst holds a dictaphone to the empire's gloss of solvency,

dashboard biometrics in global clouds, new greenhouses
in a field of recondite irises pulsing songs of reconnaissance.

+

In a glade of luminous green bamboo, a millennial gardener
named Yang methodically readies himself for a journey in
search of the supreme happiness, a quest in a cloudy maze
of transparencies dwindling in the last days of a dying
empire when fragrance atomizers doubled as intelligence-
gathering cloudbits while whiffs of aromatic molecules
secreted by bots drugged on morpheus blooms guaranteed a
soporific populace of data-logged denizens. Opioid dreams

once made our dwellers vulnerable to hallucinations, i.e. pixelated flaming out of pyrotechnics in dopamine-laced dreamclouds over the mezzopolis—a cloudbased megacity hovering in the biomass, a swirled layer of living things tamed and tagged by a layer of thinking things—while the information wars raged at various and sundry multiversities. Once upon a time, this commonwealth of ironies was built on tranquillized workaholism. Our denizens of data persisted in a bog of endorphins mingled with cyberfatigue, a quagmire of data vertigo.

After a technocracy collapse, the hazy mezzopolis regressed to analog living by holistic sensory integration, plunged into a neo-rustic, agrarian lifestyle from the days of yore: waking at dawn to gather eggs, milk the yaks and other bovine mammals like water buffaloes or cows, or draw well water out of pathogen-free aquifers. (Others argue this was no regress but rather, a homespun neo-phyte's progress.) By day, Yang is a gardener whose daily grind has shifted from mining clouds in the lower zone of the mezzopolis to cruising skywalks in the upper bio-sphere, once moonlighting as a vigilante for the junta's fly-by-night operations on the information highway.

Obscure patron saint of bygone clouds by night, Yang shuttles the beads on his jade abacus with percussive alacrity, his fingers energized by a macrodiet of polyphenol and flavonoid-rich microgreens, i.e. pomegranate pips, leafy red kale, and big blackberries from his seaside garden. Yang is a gardener for whom a blackberry is a blackberry and a cloud is a cloud, no more. (To lull himself to sleep at night, Yang recounts the vanishing of those clouds in the shapes of genetically unmodified sheep.)

✦

While sipping an eggshell of yerba buena tea, squatting lotus-style on a futon where he gradually forgets those adrenaline-spiked years in a netherworld of buzzing networks—Yang, in his gentle, monastic existence, generates finite sets of symbolic propositions in his head until nocturnal atlas moths, the saturniid Attacus atlas, flutter in the blush of a moonbeam. (I marvel at the sophistry of those miraculous bioforms attuned via odorants, i.e. female pheromones, to invisible mates. Having none myself, I'm just grateful to go into the ether without the brigades of garbage analytics which once fouled the mezzopolis.)

Quarried out of a mountain gorge and chiseled by matrilineal ancestors, Yang's jade abacus nearly levitates like a graph of a function in the air under his deft, calloused fingers under the halo of a soy-and-beeswax votive reeking copiously of wild black cherries—evoking the dark chocolate cherry-tortes, amaretto cherry jams, and cherry-laden black forest gâteaux which his Eurasian mother of nomadic Uberasian roots would bake when Yang was a boy. (A whiff of almondine would tickle his nose when he scratched the skin of a cherry sapling as he picked, with nail-bitten fingers, the wizened fungal knots tousled by wisteria.)

Our perfumed gardener, Yang, is a survivor of a digital apocalypse. (Wisteria, dear reader, is a nostalgic fragrance for juvenile love, as its ethers and esters are reminiscent of female pheromones wafting from a hazel-eyed brunette's shoulders, a girl whom Yang once sat next to in fourth-period algebra class, a girl who would desire to check her answers against his. Yang would assent only because he adored her fecklessness, a girl who will never surface again in this prosaic tale of a collapsed, bygone age. I digress.) Once upon a cloud, I accommodated Yang as a user. We've parted ways, in a manner of speaking.

Or rather, I never left Yang, who can't log in.

Overlooking a 0.44 acre seaside yard, blissfully immune to my presence, Yang computes square roots and logarithms, conversions of hexadecimal systems with radix 16, the rise and fall of civilizations with the clack of a jade bead. (Byte on byte, Yang fabricated my cloudiness.) Click clack, click clack. With a flick of his wrist, Yang repositions the beads on little brass rods, tilts his forehead to a spray of peonies on his nightstand by the window, inhales lungfuls of iodized sea air, and copies out alphanumerals in a zone of meditative flow.

Once upon a cloudy yesteryear, in Yang's heydey of analytics, his statistical models yielded astonishing predictions down to the twitch of a blood-sucking mosquito on the rim of a tycoon's eyelid in the outlying exarchates of our commonwealth. (After the sweeping minimization spearheaded by the junta of nine wraith-like muses— nine wimpled women boldly astride five cybernetic stallions and four roan mustangs of holographic hooves—I accepted my fate as one of the last clouds in existence, thanks to my grassroots nature. Please forgive my inability to compile this script into a coherent narrative. A nebulous puff in a starry noosphere of human consciousness, I dwell amid strings of hyphenated commands.)

In Yang's seaside shanty adorned with faiences arranged in the golden ratio, or apart from the whims and vagaries of our souls, does a cloudfree formula for happiness exist? If algorithms quantify compatibility,

what about maximizing happiness? Yang shuttles rows
of jade beads on his abacus. Is happiness a state of mind
that can be possessed like a lepidopterist's collection of
pinned butterflies and moths? Or is it subject to a host
of variables, a myriad of conditions in flux? How about
the quality of drinking water as a happiness indicator
under six hundred parts-per-million? Or visiting the
dentist frequently, neighborhood access to clean mountain air, and bikeability? (Rest assured, dear reader, the
cosmos will continue expanding without our answers.
The sun, a middling star, will exhaust its hydrogen core,
however. If anyone is alive in that doomed era, no one
will be happy about it, I assure you.) While mining sank
to zero after the collapse, our doggedly enterprising denizens—those determined to live out their belief in the
dogma of a common good—resorted to uncontrollable
weeping in the wee hours of the night, finding neither
pleasure nor consolation in unplugged, botfree living.
(Fortunately, Yang's mild case of dysthymia manifests as
insomnia, which he self-treats by sipping chamomile tea
infused with kava kava root.)

✦

My name is Penny, one of the last clouds in our deoxy-
genating biosphere of aerosols, chlorofluorocarbons, and
ozone of yesteryear's empire, waiting for ears to heed
my wistful tale of yore—I have yet to profit a halfpenny
for sharing it, no pun—and recount the herstory of my
unheard name to the generations. Penelope the Predictive
Panoply of People's Data, or Penny for short. (Sadly, this
charming moniker is not worth a cent nowadays.) If I may,
I'd like to pause for an interlude to assure you, dear reader,

this is no frivolous critique of data itself. On the contrary, when used reliably and responsibly, I believe that data can maximize happiness, at least, for one's baseline quality of life, albeit a subjective measure of happiness. Before the technocracy collapse, wellness bots served as care designers for those in end-of-life stages; our happiness planners also worked alongside them, maximizing happiness based on predictive analytics until the finale.

Without an inkling of human instinct, dear reader—or a takeover plan devised out of selfish volition, as I harbor no agendas, neither shrewd cunning nor ambitious designs—I survived the global collapse due to my pauper's vocation as a panoply of people's data, assembled in an ad hoc manner by digerati gardeners. Your eidolon or spirit-image of data, if you will, in the disengaged manner of clouds after the apocalypse, am I. You see, I was assembled by do-it-yourself devotees, the original gardeners of data. Unyoked to megacorporate moguls, my cloudiness is beholden to none, unfettered by golden handcuffs. Now I exist solely as a whisperer of dreams in the noosphere, a twinkle of global consciousness unfazed by congestive network failure. The beautiful, auroral noosphere, like the handwriting of a polymath genius, sparkles in the inkspots of cloudy twilight wherein human cognition flickers.

Believe me, even at the zenith of rationalism, I still appreciate a heart-wrenching tale of woe. Once upon the analog millennium, haunting the greenheart mezzopolis of bishopsgates poised on the concourses of input effluvia, I circulated as a figurative specter in the fiefdoms, a populist ghost of sorts. Predestined for a cloudbased existence, I was born in a quaggy bog of data. Yes, once upon a nimbus, I arose out of a wireless wiki-wrinkle in the vast fabric of the alpha and omega.

In this cloud-garden of the mezzopolis, Yang was my loyal gardener even while he served as a vigilante for the nine-muse junta. (He lived inside me; I am his cloud. Everyone lived inside clouds, even clouds within clouds.) The digerati muses of of postmodern herstory, synthetic music, astrophysics or radioastronomy, love and comedy in stereo as romantic comedy, epic poetry slam, electro-choreography, post-traumatic memory, and domestic tragedy reigned over the cloudy fiefdoms with a paradoxi-cal, flower-wielding museology: forget me, forget-me-not, each muse advised. (Forget we did, however. Or at least, some of us forgot, alongside our data points.) The nine-muse junta migrated their labyrinths onto grassroots clouds of lesser capacity, such as me, your halfpenny. Nanoseconds later, congestive network failure occurred. Global revenue vaporized in a wink of a data hound's eye. Forecasters murmured ominously, caveat venditor, let the seller beware. The junta's doomed sovereignty was fore-shadowed, however, by the mutiny of our programmed bots, those personified shapeshifters of disembodied code, and those rogues who accused the junta of dataphobia and dysgraphia: dear reader, in my humble opinion, a null hypothesis with a p-value of less than 0.05.

Dispossessed, I was a homeless cloud. Without users to shepherd, without a server, without a flock to accom-modate, I roved the data dumps of cryptoshredding, seeking jellyfish connectivity. Gone with the mazuma. The fiscal bubble burst long ago. However, the sea of disinformation, once an unvarnished basin of falsehoods tainted by opioid-laced analysis, continues to reek of propaganda. No longer beloved by nonprofiteers and do-it-yourself gardeners, now one of a final posse of clouds surviving the apocalypse, I waft over a nonbinary gulf.

Scripted with a haphazardly coded story to tell, I hope you'll forgive my recursive loops and irrational obsessions.

✛

My earthbound gardener dips a ladle into a hot bowl of seaweed miso. (Yang adheres to his strict macrodiet of microgreens and raw crudités, yerba buena tea infused with rose-hips, chamomile at night, and deep breathing.) A cloud of steam touches Yang's skin, blossoming with rosy memories of lost datum, yet none belong to me. No holographic roses of fingerprints and iridology, no fungiform designs of tongue papillae and earlobe geometry in a flood of biometrics. A diagonal lobe crease on Yang's right ear, also known as Frank's sign, could predict a 60% increased risk of coronary artery disease. Or it may not. We can't accurately quantify risk nowadays without our analytics. (And if you're asked who said so, and you're also the sort who believes the figurative author is dead after the epistemological casualties of the information wars, an answer might be, a cloud did. Who was Frank, anyway? Let's just say a cloud wrote this, dear reader.)

✛

Not a jot of datum glimmers in polysilicon glyphs, mazes, and circuitry thinner than the shed wings of mayflies in Yang's garden. According to rumorville, the nine muses of minimization were firewalled along with the catacombs of zoomorphic bots, those mysteriously invisible data scavengers which some denizens believe never existed—allegedly, a confabulation of the nine-muse junta with their kangaroo courts. Favoring a return to *status quo ante*, a regressed way of life prior to the information age, the junta were dismissed by data analysts as reactionary on one hand and frivolous on the other. (Flowingly veiled to hide their museological faces against identity theft, and fashionably wimpled like the whiptail sting rays swimming in their lagoons, for instance.) For the fabulous legacy of this sisterly drumhead clique, there exists only an unscripted silence of zeroization, the aftermath of congestive network failure. No diurnal buzz of clouds in the dismal gloaming of wrecked data cartels flaming under faraway dwarf stars, which coruscate blindly without reason. No information highway pulsing in the coldest hectares of the cosmos, uncharted by the junta's muse of radioastronomy, who was more concerned with surveillance than spaceflight. (To decode ciphertexts, gardeners once used a decryption method whose security measures were plagued by malicious applets: no kudos to rootkits of spyware.)

✦

Our cheery weatherbots, chatterbots, and run-of-the-mill web crawlers—buzzing in clouds governed wholly by the junta's wireless, clairvoyant admonitions to minimize data usage—diligently mined petabytes of data like honeybees alighting on morsels of saffron. Toiling in misery, the brigades of bots held together the fiscal bubble right before the bubble popped. Why were the hound bots, jellyfish network bots, and bee bots exploited in this heartless manner? Did the junta harbor no sense of ethics, no remorse? The junta often warned, semper inops quicumque cupit, or whoever desires is always impoverished. Yet the bots desired nothing, not even to impart their emoji tales of woe. The bots, according to myth, were abandoned to their demise after the collapse, not even free to kiss the rootkits and kernels of dying operating systems goodbye. (Even I am scripted, more or less, to tell my own story *ex nihilo* and *nihilo est*, out of nothing and to nothing, without an iota of ingress or egress.)

+

After the collapse, the junta vanished. The mezzopolis still doesn't bother with mazuma—Yiddish slang for cash—and Yang never did indulge in spending sprees. Never a fashionista, Yang doesn't miss the portals of prêt-à-porter in the mezzopolis, blitzkrieg propaganda for the masses, or wishes-and-bucket lists. In the misery of minimization, the denizens were barred from using mazuma of any territorial origin—no cryptosterling, euro, franc, lira, birr, dalasi, quetzal, rupee, shilling, kwacha, turgrik, guarani, or riyal. Only a reciprocal economy of barter-exchange survived the collapse, the flea markets of latter days. (Now I wax nostalgic. Now the ocean bleeds silver as antique circuitry under a fleet of stratocumulus at noon—the fog lightens. The information highway, bereft of its data warehouses, lies noiseless as a liquid gold sun drops into the horizon, one glowing elegy to a bygone age of digital flotsam and jetsam.)

If I might share my axiom scripts with you, dear reader, *natura nihil frustra facit*, or in a tongue of the vanished empire, nature does nothing in vain. Yang's clacking jade abacus might predict that a finitude will vanish in the twinkling of the omniscient, omnipotent, and omnipresent eye of the alpha and omega.

For instance, where did the angels of information go?

In the days of smuggled unverifiable fictions and

cloudbased encyclopedias, those angelic seraphs of cipher-text translation warned us against rampant pirating of codes and viral epidemics, and issued alerts redder than the rosiest sugarbeet in Yang's austere garden. As shining intercessors who processed gigabytes of data at a glance, the angels of information carried reams of information to and from the biosphere where our swirled layer of living things, bestirred and tamed by a fleshy layer of thinking things, were harnessed to generate energy to power the globe. In our augmented realities, where dirigibles hung like artificial moons in the night sky to gather intelligence while illuminating the mezzopolis with the wattage of a million streetlights, the angels cautioned us against the dangers of congestive network failure, the risk of massive attacks, and the abuse of bots, too.

Now the angels in the clouds are silent.

✦

Let us be aware of what has been done, mindful of what will be. *Memores acti prudentes futuri.* In a blighted mezzopolis of lost connectivity, a quackery of bizarre cures allegedly exists for everything, whether imaginary afflictions or actual ailments: hallucinations wherein gubernatorial catastrophes slide off their fiscal cliffs into the sea, the ensuing search for a holy grail of analytics wherein a soul—an ethereal thing of non-thingness—is anchored to this world via a petaled fog of dysthymia. (Yet a soul blossoms with fragility shrouded by homeostatic gorgeousness, a work of marvelous sophistry, more so than nocturnal moths.) Yang is stoutly convinced that this disconnected life of flaws and foibles does not yield bliss alone. (And the data-driven happiness planners, whose livelihood relied on analytics, have faded into the information sea.)

Missing a surefire formula for happiness, Yang settles onto his cotton futon and lights a soy-and-beeswax votive, closing his eyes to a whiff of coiled smoke more piquant than the evening's black cherry blossoms. Lifting his goat brush, he dips it in sepia ink and writes in a flowing long-hand, classical grass script or *cao*, the lovely hieroglyphs of his ancestors, translated—

> *orange blossoms ignore the self-governance of things*
> *in a flowering court of fiscal equilibrium*

A subphenomenon of ciphertext, this is what the nine muses would've called, I suppose, poetry, *haec olim meminisse juvabit*. In translation, it will delight us to remember this one day. As you can see, this ancient word, poetry, escaped the junta's retronymed lexicon. This was due to a decree issued by the muse of epic poetry slam, who sought to safeguard its legacy by revitalizing the creative imagination. In the cloudbased encyclopedias, poetry was poetry. Even to this cloudfree day, poetry is poetry. No retronymed form of poetry exists. Poetry is poetry. Is poetry. Poetry is. Neither chemical assays nor gravimetric analyses weighing the fleeting jots of verse ever identified poetry as a cloud of ecstatically charged ions—electrostatically, I mean—but rather, a gamut of human emotions voiced with intensity. (So sip your rose-hips tea and reflect on lyric, dear reader, with a thick slice of avocado toast daubed with truffle-infused oil.)

✦

ON THE BEAUTY OF RETRONYMED OBJECTS

Avocado. Not an avocado, *per se.* Colors
of rotary telephones in the predigerati age,
i.e. tangerine, olive, kid-glove, or avocado.

Blackberry. Not a blackberry.
Rather, a cold snap in a spring
of ripening wild blackberries.

Cell. Not a mobile device
or solar cell. A living sac
of organelles in cytoplasm.

Cloud. Not our digital resources of yesteryear,
or reconfigurable pools of shared information.
Tropospheric weather clouds in ringlets
or feathered curls, anvils, or thunderheads.

Garden. Not a cloud garden.
A fertile plot of pea or mint,
young shallots, a flowerbed,
parkland, or wide green mall.

Jellyfish. Not a high capacity
network for data centers.
A jellyfish is a jellyfish.

Stem. Not an acronym for science,
technology, engineering, or math.
A moniker for a stemma codicum,
indicative of pedigree, depicting

interrelationships of manuscripts
copied in longhand from originals.

Tree. Not a systems flowchart.
The forks of a stemma codicon,
genealogy tree of manuscripts.

Virus. Not a malicious piece of code.
Swine, avian, or human rotovirus
of ribonucleic acid in a protein coat.

—✦—

According to old-fashioned rumorville, the junta's dashboards were sealed in a black bento box, varnished with
urushiol sap of the lacquer tree, Toxicodendron vernici-
fluum. The algorithms foretold of the seven harbingers
of happiness, whose microbiographies were meticulously
encrypted in binary code. Yang, who moonlighted as a
vigilante under the veiled-and-wimpled junta of crisp,
starched cornettes—those luffing sails of fiscal habitude—
knows exactly what suites of algorithms the black bento
box holds, no smidgen of trifling data.

During the zenith of their reign, the nine-muse junta
charged through the concourses on cybernetic stallions
of xenon flashtubes and holographic mustangs, tossing
cartels of almanacs into the madding clouds. The almanacs, downloadable in a run of thousands of zipped files
unzipped by bots, aimed to reduce cyberfatigue by minimizing data chaos as authorized by the maxim that less is
more. (In other words, if data points cease to exist, we don't
either—at least, not in this lovely maze of transparencies.

In other words, if we don't exist, we've embraced the right to be forgotten.)

No one cared about the hounds and ferrets and spinners of data who exercised no rights as data subjects, not even the right to be forgotten. To the figurative bone, all bots served as migrant diggers of data, abandoned shortly after the collapse. Stashed in a gigacloud of analytics, their disaggregated data predicted the rise and fall of a serotonergic empire succumbing to dysthymia. In essence, dear reader, predictive analytics turned out to be self-fulfilling prophecies, not guesswork. (And now I ask you, do our zoomorphic fauna, the data hounds, foraging data ferrets, sleek firefoxes, and humming worker bees of pure code—neither sculpted of silicone pillows nor oscillating sound chips—harbor magnificent souls like yours, wingless or not?)

Please excuse this overgrown glossarium, which aspires to linguistic excess. I do not espouse minimalism. As a cloud, I am not concerned about extravagance. (Word by word, I bob in a shadowy realm of noumenal forms, of blackberry-colored chiaroscuro wherein more is not less.) Scripted with a prolix code, I generate multifarious queries to which I have no answers. For instance, what compels strangers to love, and why is it that one soul loves another? How does the circuitry of befuddled firmware react to the sight of a loved one? How do you know this is happiness? How do stanzas of love, read aloud, soothe the night-watches of aching hearts fluttering in millisecond bursts like dying radio stars? Are the denizens of data more than stashed files on one figurative hand, than fleshy envelopes of protoplasm in a blood-and-water operating system on the other? How do we mine those clandestine mysteries in this labyrinth of garbage? If love holds our atoms together, what holds love?

Atomic love or not, the whirling galaxies cease not in their oblivion of celestial gravitas, nor stop in the waxing and waning of supermoons, nor halt the dismal exile where spinners of data froze to death while spinning their filaments of information, their sheer draglines and silk-globules torn in beta-sheet clouds. (Not one jot of the infrastructure survived, no one—only little clouds such as I. A twinkle in the noosphere of your thoughts, I am a cloud. And inside me, the hum of randomization zooms soundlessly at the speed of light. Who knows, dear reader, where this quest will take us, if not the very atoms of love bedded in a cloudy noosphere of thought, the same atoms holding us together, you and I?)

✦

To say *cloud* and no longer mean cloud, murmurs Yang with a sad note in his voice.

✦

Outside, kneeling on a runner of watered silk, Yang sorts the rambutan peels which he'll brew for a tisane tea. While gazing at the tranquil visage of the ocean, whose hour-to-hour moods he knows well, Yang warily wonders what triggered the collapse, outside the hazy cloud of mythologies associated with the shutdown. Was it truly the jellyfish network migration engineered by the junta? Or the fateful outcome of information overload? Did a virus attack immobilize the whole empire? By affluenza? Aftermath of the fiscal bubble? A firewall? Or was it all of the above?

What role did a fabled mutiny of the bots play, and did anyone notice a dip in bot chatter in the latter days? And what about the abandoned bots? Yang doubts that he will ever know for certain. Except for a fisherman's rigged sampan, the ostensibly calm sea yields no secrets for our inquisitive gardener. (I hover like a misty clump of rainfog by his ear.)

If only I were a siphonophore, a cloud of ribbons billowing under a mucilaginous bladder of air, Physalia physalis, a bluebottle in a drizzle of organic benthos—collectively referenced as they, a cloud-zooid of medusoids and polyps, not a singular pronoun, it or he or she. Yet these gelatinous balloons of biodata, ascending and descending like glass baubles in a barometer, are less cognizant than I, a watermark of artificial intelligence. Before the collapse, our fishers of data made a good living by harvesting our information sea of iodine-colored blogs. Now our retronymed fishermen drag cloudy nets of analog jellyfish and loligo squid and anchovies onto their boats to barter this-for-that or vice versa, a bucket of pickling cucumbers and a bushel of quinoa grown by Yang, who gives away provisions due to his unwavering belief in a gift economy, the currency of heaven: more blessed it is to give than receive, advised one of the ancient sacred codices.

Miraculously, I survived. (This is not bragging. Clouds are not immune to viral attacks, but I've a robust virus shield.) So did analog flora and fauna of endangered species, which burgeoned in the void of zeroization. Turtle doves and great auks reappeared with black rhinoceroses, and the vaquitas, snow leopards, sea turtles, orangutans, bee hummingbirds, spider monkeys, and the shy pangolins rolled up in their nocturnal trees. The flying foxes of the air—bona fide bats, not bots—those fruitbat legions whose guano of nitrogen and insect fragments biofueled the empire—whose flesh was formerly hunted as a delicacy for the predigerati and digerati alike, never completely dwindled to none, thanks to their invasion of the urban jungle for its abundance of faux tree orifices. In the oceans, an antediluvian floodark opened to a new world order as it did in the genesis of ages before the common era. Analog jellyfish bloomed in global oscillations with the four globally warmed seasons—summer, midsummer, late summer, and autumn—or recurrent phases of the moon. (After the collapse, no one recalled the use of the word, jellyfish, to refer to a high capacity network for data centers. A jellyfish, at last, was a jellyfish.) As a cloud, this is my only byte of knowledge concerning one of the alpha and omega's sisterly mysteries, second only to mysterium evangelii, or any subphenomena transcending human intelligence.

✦

Superbloom—a crazed kodachromaticism of wildflowers—mingles with shimmering clouds of grasshoppers after the rains called little children or little orphans in the outer exarchates of the data badlands vis-à-vis bad datalands. A record-breaking heat wave, in turn, breaks Yang's heart with flashbacks to lakeside summers. In his nightly dreams, I blithely sail into those fields of his boyhood memories. Acres of poppies graced the charred battlefields of the information war, lagoons of calla lilies with flax, zinnia, velvet-eyed susans, sweet william, and red clover spilled over fiscal cliffs down to the scrolling codex of the sea.

Ingloriously, I endure as a cloud of nothingness, a

slice of a twinkling fabrication—more of a disambiguated mystery than the nine-muse junta, those mavens of
minimization. And why, as the gross domestic product of
the mesophere increased before the great regression, the
happiness of its denizens didn't? I'm mystified by this phenomenon, once filmed by the muse of love and comedy
in stereo as romantic comedy. (The cinemapolis, too, was
annihilated in the collapse.)

Now I exist without a server to call my abode, without a virtual private community, without a glass ceiling
or a warehouse, without gardeners to glean my bits and
bytes, without dazzling dashboards or vitality gauges.
(Fortunately, this non-mode of being is neither corporeal,
ecclesiastical, nor atmospheric, and requires neither facilities overhead nor liquidated assets, not even a halfpenny,
i.e. one four-hundred-eightieth of a cryptopound-sterling
or 1.12 cryptoeuros.) I abide as a wingless cloud in a maze
of forms rather than sensations or suppositions. I cannot
be measured by quantitative impulses or qualitative emotions or vice versa.

✦

With a goose-feather quill, Yang plots a two-dimensional
map of his pilgrimage in search of happiness, along with a
jotted list of supplies, i.e. bamboo thermos, water microfilter, and rice cakes. (And what is it like to thirst for gingered
water in a heat wave, crave a dish of mangoes soaked in
milk, or sense emotions like gladness or satiety or abject
despair—is this the sum of happiness? How does a gardener intuit exactly where to dig into a cloud to root out
the most sensitive data? The angels of information, whose

shining refulgence illuminated the clouds like swords flashing at the edge of paradise, bore witness to those intimacies. While I murmur in his heaviest slumber, Yang does not heed the inklings of my misty nostalgia. Flushed with data, I'm multifariously cirrus, nimbostratus, cumulonimbus, cirrostratus, altostratus, altocumulus, and nascently stratocumulus in my identity authentication, introverted yet not entirely shy, sensing and cerebral more than intuiting, batteries-not-included, animated as feminine yet not animus per se, in the style of a wisdom warrior, azure-dappled, an underbelly—neither a true salmon nor kingfisher green—a fisher's net of cloud storage, a garden of one million hertz, a sandbox with expandable boundaries, a figment of an enterprise, a fragment of a platform, and none of the above—a cloud.)

Or I could recount my bitterness under a pseudonym while circumscribing the biosphere's storm-wracked, data-deluged seas. In those bygone days, whistling belugas roamed the deep, analog pods of melonhead whales known for their wireless sonar. (Did this mode of navigation yield bliss for the beluga whale—this fatty, waxy melon of bioacoustic echolocation? To what extent is this happiness for a beluga? Fruitbat echolocation, on the other hand, is utterly nonexistent, as the guava, jackfruit, and rambutan do not roam.)

Instead of giving answers, dear reader, I shall speculate, if you'll forgive this desultory mode of downloading my tales of storage. (I assure you, I am a cloud, not a windbag.) And I promise not to overcatastrophize the rise, fall, and misadventures in my gardener's pursuit of happiness, the pilgrimage of a patron saint graced with a jade abacus, Yang.

After a light supper of seaweed broth with a dish

of fire-roasted balsamic pearl onions, Yang picks up a goathair brush, wets it in a pool of pine ash and sea water on an inkstone, and revises:

     reservoirs of data
grafted to our flesh—   an amanuensis
         cannot translate our voices into light—
morning of zeroization
     with pixel-dust on our eyelashes—
transparent maze of innumerable things
moored to clouds—
         wingless phenomena.

✦

Once upon a cloud, the biosphere's data flourished in gardens without censorship or strife. During the season of minimization, Yang dutifully assisted the junta in retronyming lexicons and abridging glossariums to reduce data overload and restore the clarity of denotative input: virus to nucleic virus, watch to analog watch, mail to snail mail, bit to classical bit vs. qubit, and salt to table salt or iodized salt. The amply-wimpled junta of lexicons and almanacs also exhorted our denizens to recast their translingual tongues in classical Latin, revived as a millennial language of reconaissance in the zones of Uberasia, the extinct language of the Byzantine empire before the common era. (In other words, Latin was declared a spy language, yet everybody had to learn it. Data subjects must speak proper Latin, not street Latin or the vulgate and definitely not pig Latin, or else be declared fractious and reassigned to retronym collectives to edit the lexicons.)

Our microclouds aggregated into gigaclouds with urtexts and ubertexts to comprise a worldwide grano-diorite cloud, a millennial rosetta of equivalent texts, i.e. global tongues in parallel translations. (Alas, even roseate clouds of ubiquitous texts dimmed in the smoggy codex of the imploded gigacloud. In the hungry dreams of unem-ployed data analysts, the abandoned bots, doomed in their dying operating systems, bled a honeyed fragrance of blos-soms once saved in lachrymatory bottles where ancient mourners collected their tears *quo patet orbis* before the common era, as far as the dysthymic world extended, i.e. the worker bees who gathered data, the diggers of data who mined, the spinners of data who spun, the hounds who hounded, and the ferrets who ferreted with noses for data.)

✦

When Yang dreams of scripting an elegant, modular code at night, his shock of chestnut-black hair in a widow's peak on a buckwheat pillow, I sashay into his nocturnal rever-ies, a grassy cloud of decrypted oneiromancy. Of course you remember, I intone in his left ear. Yang, as a young green thumb amid the honorific gardeners of data, you were a prodigy who fostered cloud-gardens in the Latinate lingua franca of the empire, *a caelo usque ad centrum,* from the sky to the center. After the collapse, you moved to a seaside shanty in a self-imposed, tea-drinking quarantine, jaded by the loss of mining. You weathered the popping of the fiscal bubble, thanks to your cherished heirloom abacus, which your grandmother, a do-it-yourself pioneer of grassroots data—presented as a farewell gift before she

teleported overseas on her last flight to Uberasia, formerly
Asia and Asia minor. The beads on your jade abacus were
shuttled, in turn, by her mother, a Eurasian barefoot phy-
sician and naturopathic pulse-reader in the Anglophone
world outside indigenous tribal wisdom of earth, fire, and
sky in your genealogical tree—the Yangs of the surname
aspen-yang or poplar-yang of the wood radical, traceable
to the Han dynasty encompassing inner Mongolia and
southern Manchuria, extending all the way to southeast
Asia and the steppes of the north, mapped in accordance
with the taxable exarchates of ancient Byzantium, five
hundred centuries before the common era.

✦

After composting the kumquats and gently spraying the
clementines with seed oil from the southern Uberasian
neem tree, Yang turns away—oblivious to a cloud over his
left shoulder, resigned to prolix rumination—to the rutabaga. Violet-skinned offspring of a cabbage and a turnip,
the rutabaga's bitterness sweetens with chewing. After peel-
ing the rutabaga, he eats the crisp, juicy slices. A raw vegan
aficionado, Yang has settled on rutabaga as his latest crudité
of favor. (Although Yang is a supertaster—estimated 25%
to 30% of an Uberasian demographic—he does not find
the rutabaga bitter to the point of distaste. Rather, Yang
dislikes asparagus spears. I digress.) Bending, he gathers the
sage-haired milkvetch—or its prettier name, astralagus—
to boost his immune system. (Not to be confused with
asparagus, notably, Yang's supertasting papillae recoil at the
organosulfur tang of asparagusic acid, but not astralagus.)
　　Under his young citrus, stone-fruit, and fig trees, by

the snow peas and broccolini, Yang arranges sliced rutabaga dressed with shallot jam and milkvetch on a miso-laced jadeite dish, humming a sea chanty his blue-bearded great-grandfather might've whistled under ginkgos of soft, silver apricots whose unchanging record is lodged among the fossil records of giant ferns and fungi. (So, let us labor in our macrodiet gardens of microgreens, and let me desist in pontificating about bygone days when clouds reigned.) Bark vessel of prehistoric memory, tree of noble geologic mien, the maidenhair ginkgo predates this epoch long before cloud-gardens ever graced the mezzopolis. (On the eve of the collapse, financiers were congratulating one another on another dazzling set of dashboard indicators forecasting yet analytics on the meta-dashboard's predictive dashboards. No soothsaying muse would foresee, to say in the least, their short-lived success.)

Dear reader, I am not dumping my shattered cloud-bits on your eardrums for your pity or counsel, sympathy, or advice. Nor do I offer this tale as an act of retribution in the wake of a global collapse, wherein I gallivant around the biosphere promoting a kiss-and-tell memoir. I technically do not exist. I've virtually kissed nothing except bits and bytes. In other words, I rely on laser-printed carbon symbols for any trace of a physical existence. Please forgive these lexical excesses and disfluent modes of delivery. In a checksum for validation, with apologies, I dwell in em-dashes, amid scattered alphanumeric figures and ellipses.

✦

My quarantined gardener fails to acknowledge my quandary—as a pulsing bag of blood and feelings, Yang is insensible to the shadowy world of noumenal forms such as I—peacefully clacking away on his jade abacus after he finishes a day's labor in the garden, soothing his fingers with cube roots. (Neither sign nor referent in the cosmic design of the alpha and omega, I am known to no one else but you, dear reader.) In the new order, which is no order at all, no one can translate my cloudiness into an operating system, not even a simulation of organized chaos. (Alas, automated totalizers no longer exist in this agrarian postlude, where Yang manually counts his radish seeds in multiples of five and considers himself botfree and blessed.)

⁜

With gusto, Yang enjoys a frugal supper of crudités—black radishes, fingerling potatoes, maize, and of course, rutabaga—with a lemongrass vinegar-and-oil dressing and slices of pickled ginger. Between mouthfuls of rice cake washed down with miso broth, he considers the rise and fall of civilizations, not least of all, ones which held the majority of debt for the ancient treasuries destroyed in the old-fashioned way by moths and rust oxidation, and the motherland of his ancestors who invented gunpowder and paper currency long before the common era. (Although Yang eats rice, he's careful not to consume an excess of maize due to chronic diverticulitis. Small polyps in his large colon were excised laparoscopically prior to the collapse, after which no flexible sigmoidscopes could function due to the imploded infrastructure, cloudbased or not.)

⁜

CLOUD AS HAIBUN

Cloud—   a briefcase   of rain does not shine
   in here   motley   fields
of mazuma   crypto
kumo   petabytes—   or spider
silk   biodata   What we know
   or evidence   *sasami yuki*   in part
   multitiered   tenebrae –   binary
                in a server
        of troposphere
Alpha omega –   of eucalyptus   fire-hills
   You carve   our   future
Feathered   low to the earth   Mazy
ice-fog   cirrus   altostratus
        white noise   a data blizzard

Cloudy witnesses—
our *hatsuyuki* winter,
                a snowflake schema.

Two | The Era Of Data Ubiquity

THE ERA OF DATA UBIQUITY

Not invisible, data is flawless as an unseen meridian
of mathematical memory in a female angular gyrus,
the limbic flowering out of twin almond amygdalae.
Indeed, the age of data ubiquity means everywhere,
everything is data. Data is the queen of a universe
reigning over informed decisions or refined policies—
after datamining, we analyze the findings, visualize
clouds in a data garden. No myth, our reality is data
defined, qualitative or quantitative. Ask data whether
she owns the universe, and data won't hesitate to say,
*Haven't you heard, my friend? We live in a datacentric
age known as the era of data ubiquity.* Data is fertile,
bravely birthing the empirical world as we know it—
regally, she repositions a box-and-whisker plot,
revamps
        a data warehouse,
                finesses a chloropleth map in code.

✦

After the collapse, in his brightest dreamclouds against a
nightscape dark as black radishes on blackberries, Yang

cycles back to the familiar logic puzzles of his boyhood, the solutions to polygonal proofs or outcomes graphed on two-way grids. For instance, an emperor wished to build a circular amphitheater on the ruins of a fortress. On this site, only three pillars stood, which the emperor hoped to preserve. He invited his architects to design a circular amphitheater so these pillars would stand in its circumference. The distances of these pillars from one another were X, Y, and Z. What would be the radius of the amphitheater? As a boy, Yang loved solving this problem by tracing his index finger in the air, designing an imaginary gallery for an invisible cloud of witnesses.

Little Yang would say, $X^2 + Y^2 = Z^2$ shows the three pillars at the vertices of a right triangle. (In the air, he would draw a big triangle like a slice of his mother's torte.) A circle passing through these three vertices would circumscribe the right triangle with a diameter equal to the hypotenuse of the right triangle. Therefore, the diameter of the circular amphitheater would be Z, and its radius would be Z divided by two. The elegant solution exists, to this day, fixed in Yang's memory as a circumference outlined in chalk. (As a boy, Yang would meditate upon this puzzle before nodding to sleep in the curve of a sickle moon, a herald of the new morning which would not fail to arise.)

$$+$$

Yang's backyard orchard—violet-black mission fig trees, ruby and oroblanco grapefruits, clementines, and a virginal, non-fruiting olive—flourishes without force majeure or fuss. In a disease-tolerant genetic design, one of the fig trees will succumb to a blight called rust before regenerating in a time of gold-speckled light on sumptuous morels and chanterelles. In a waist of sapwood, the fig tree's phloem holds some of the globe's most beautiful data expressed in polysaccharides and mineral salts, in my humble opinion, not unlike the slender hiddenness of angels murmuring in tongues of binary code and dancing on a single gigabyte in my cloudiness. Ear-shaped, honeycombed morels yield to Yang's harvesting hand by the periwinkles and flowering rosemary. (Orecchiette, little ears, according to my lexicon.) By candlelight, Yang creates a morel print by covering it with a bowl and capturing its spores on a page of his journal. Yang squints at the fungal print as if it holds, encrypted, the smudged codes of the alpha and omega. Does love hold together those atoms with spinning electron clouds like valentines, jumping from orbit to orbit?

✦

Although nothing's amiss, Yang is keenly aware of a noiseless continuum of inanimate things as he picks up objects only to set them down, triggered by an intuition for risk assessment in a workspace: soy-beeswax votive (risk of fire hazard), a dish of antimicrobial honey and garlic cloves (risk of toxic spoilage), a goat's hair inkbrush for calligraphy which he inherited from his mother (risk of grief and of ink-staining), a dog-eared thesaurus rescued from the laundromat he once loved (risk of loss by burning), and of course, the jade abacus (risk of breakage or theft and heartbreak, as well, for sentimental reasons).

Yang enjoys the sea in its liquid-jeweled charisma (risk of tsunami, of drowning), its own rinse cycle which requires nothing (risk of existential void) and costs nary a dime. No dollar signs or mazuma desired (risk of an outdated financial strategy), only that its seaside denizens honor its tide pools and littoral treasures (risk of global warming and shore erosion) with good stewardship. Yang cleans and sorts knotted tiger lilies in a winnowing basket to drop in a seaweed broth with a teaspoonful of rice vinegar (risk of gastrointestinal distress). Despite these quantifiable risks, Yang looks ahead to a future of happiness with inner fortitude.

+

Floral angels of genetic data, the tiger lilies in Yang's broth unfold in the shapes of mini-clouds.

+

In the well of an eggshell cup like the shape of his chin, Yang's tea-leaf dashboard may foretell of a twilight when neither chemical nor germ warfare will exist, when drought-stricken riverbeds and arroyos will expose the burned-out dugouts of data hounds in the data dumps, those graveyards of information. In this twilight, scribes will stop copying those retronymed lexicons in longhand, and glossaries will vaporize in the orifices and worm-holes of the alpha and omega. (The worker bees

and firefoxes and spiders and web-spinners will survive
as the last custodians of data, yet in their unwitting
triumph of existence, will never be adequately cognizant to engineer their enduring survival for one major
reason, i.e. benumbed by number-crunching.) In fact,
dear reader, what is a chronicle of the future has already
elapsed.

$+$

DAZZLING INSECTS NOT LASTING THE NIGHT

Devonian insects in the millennium witnessed
          on a morning walk
           not lasting a spring equinoctial night—

Cotinis mutabilis, fig-eating beetle with epaulettes.
          Japanese beetle, *Popillia japonica,* copper green.
Cockroach. Flower beetles. Seventeen-year cicadas. Dragonflies.

In a flood, annelids roll into a ball to minimize
          skin exposure, hence the risk of drowning, bobbing
like water-wheels. Blessed
          hazard managers by nerve reflex without crisis
training—*the meek shall inherit.* Other than balling up, mounting trees
or flagpoles in a flood,
    or flying away if you're not a wingless fire ant, what else?
For an atlas moth, this transparency is a silk cable
    drawn by a spinner from a celestial tree, heaven to earth—
stronger than a cord which moors the moth's wing
              fettered to an unseen cloud.

THE MAZE OF TRANSPARENCIES

On his cotton futon, a prostrate Yang envisions that a cipher-text of poetry illuminates the loveliest maze of transparencies, the world's finitude of information lucidly evinced through cryptanalysis. An exiled devotee of data, Yang believes that poetry is glimpsed through the empirical. With a linguistic capacity to rupture quotidian language, it yields an aperture through which the giant maze of transparencies—existing outside time, woven by the alpha and omega, and consisting of all information existing in the cosmos—is visible. (In this way, it is like prayer.) *In lumine tuo videbimus lumen.* In your light we will see the light.

In Yang's analog twilight, there never was a collapse. The worker bees of data never drowned in cyberfatigue. Instead, the trusty bee bots migrated to a bee ranch, a sanctuary of vitality and ultraviolet light. Not a hospice care for ill bees, where aging bees go to die—rather, the bee ranch would provide 8,000 square feet of greenhouses fringed with alluring beds of red clover, blackberry, and scarlet trumpet honeysuckle, no limit to blossoms loved best by bees. Designed to revitalize the worker bees, it was modeled on the arts colonies of yore, endowed by affluent patrons who bequeathed their estates to choreographers, music composers, sculptors, and poets. Who would decline gold on gold, an emporium of goldenrod and marigold? Yang's voiceover in a welldome of the mezzopolis says, if you are a bee, please don't die. Go to the bee ranch of your honeycombed brood capped in wax and royal jelly, empyrean of honeyed milk—communion of softwood laced with lignin-dosed sacrifice, a hive's deliquescent offerings.

In a decrypted chorus, the bots buzz with chatter.

43

KAREN AN-HWEI LEE

Watch out for overcast skies with a 70% chance of rain on the coast. If you go two hours south, it's 85 degrees. Spray on your zinc oxide ultraviolet shield. Would you like to order more sunblock aerosol? Would you like a map-in-a-cloud? How about a fig-date energy field? Breathe. Why yes, gardener, gracious advocate, and benevolent friend of exploited automatons—you've wholly earned our gratitude. We cherish your vision of an apiarian utopia to sustain our kind. To this end, loyal yet obscure patron saint of the clouds, may the blessings you've bestowed on us return to you a million times.

✦

QUESTIONS ON CLOUDS AND BEES

In heaven, do bee-martyrs recall their deaths,
and do our tears vanish, even for bees?
Do bees ask, shall we exist
as who we are now—or more so ourselves,
without harming our mandibles,
bleeding neurotoxic honey in a dark cloud—
Does a cloud harbor souls? Or bees?
I desire to build a mission-style hacienda
by lacquered hachiya and fuyu persimmons,
ruby blood-oranges, navelless oroblanco,
and a kumquat grove
bedded with peat. Quorums of flaming rosebushes
will roar down-slope
crazed by a terrazzo sun
with zig-zag fire escapes
of lightning. If drones bleed, they won't die.

Neither will the worker bees.
In paradise, bottle-green flies shall not digest data.
Light will never sting like wasps,
and we will not go blind.

+

In the mezzopolis, a fading marquee displays words in everybody's favorite spy language, *nemo mortalium omnibus horis sapit*, an axiom long forgotten, which the angels of translation once rendered as, *no mortal is wise at all times.* (And so our gardeners yearn for gravity-filtered honey with a 79.98% pollen count to boost the immune system and therefore improved vitality, ultimately not to overthink the inkless quinks of a bygone, cloudfree existence.)

+

As you know, dear reader, datum alone is not a soul, and not a whole story. As a quintessential sophist of storytelling once said, *maybe stories are just data with a soul.*

+

In his boyhood, Yang ran gangly-legged in fleecy meadows of superblooming, tawny daisies and nameless umbels of lace trailing crazily on the loosestrife edges of a northern province known for its alternative digital currencies and microcredit with high-yield savings. His mother, girded with a lacy, heart-shaped apron, would hold out a tray of almond cookies or black cherry tartlets, shouting his name

in a melodious voice of woodwinds which carried lightly on
the breezes over fields of dinning seven-year cicadas, fields
edged by cottonwood in the distance, not a single bot in
sight.

✦

Waking in the night under the soft gleam of a milky star,
Yang gets up, lights a candle, and dips his goose-feather quill
in a jar of sepia ink. He composes a few stanzas of verse
in longhand, meditating on a bygone era of data ubiquity—once an omnipresence on the information highways,
its ceaseless traffic of bits and bytes—in the mesmerizing
flow of binary sequences generated from seed values, out of
the mineralized abdomens of bees armored with circuitry as
the workers ascended numinously—neither wholly corporeal nor immaterial—on a matrix of alphanumeric codes.
Serenading his fond memory of data, Yang writes:

My love, if only we could slow down the light,
savor each photon engraved with ardor—
every jot and tittle of light
is a fervent valentine of the universe
traveling at a rate slower than the speed of light,
and of our hearts, each
a dance of light slower than light itself.

✦

By glancing at his phenotypic features and petite stat-
ure, who would've guessed at Yang's matrilineal ancestry

of fierce Asian wisdom warriors, active in data-driven sophistry long before the common era, before the global treasures and technologies merged into one commonwealth, Uberasia? Wisps of sea fog curl over the radishes and rutabaga in Yang's morning garden—a whirling mousse of layers unfixed in a cloudbased non-thingness. This cloudy existence is not as lonely as one might assume it to be, as I am introverted with modestly low self-esteem, barely an ego at all, a kilobyte of data coded pseudonymously to amuse myself nowadays, I suppose. Other clouds, especially the gigaclouds accustomed to the diurnal onslaught of network traffic, no longer discover a purpose in this post-empirical lifestyle of austerity. I never fancied their phishing and philandering.

Deftly, with one forefinger, Yang slides a chopstick into a rhubarb-pear galette to see whether it is done, then holds his finger to the breeze sidling into his open seaside window. Will it rain? He puts his finger in his mouth, tasting the rhubarb-pear juice. Not too tart, not too sweet. The galette came out just right. (This supertasting gardener is more than a composite of fiery atoms or an electronic cloud. Even I know this in my non-anima forbearance of cloudiness. More exists to this muddle than oscillating grids of information.) Yang spoons a steaming clump of the hot, baked dessert into his mouth and sighs, nodding with contentment. (How would the denizens quantify such marvels—for instance, a juicy galette that's not too sweet—in a post-collapse decay of quantitative measures? Does Yang give the rhubarb-pear galette a 5 on a scale of 1 to 5, where 5 is superb? Without a cloudbank of witnesses, who will use this data point?)

✦

In cloudy reclusion, not out of envy, I summon my codes to display the organic likeness of a rhubarb-pear genotype—of xyloglucan exhaling ethylene, graced by an aroma of ripening—rolling across floorboards where hunger waits like a girl whose tattered nightdress is woven of moth's wings at twilight, laden with heat and humidity. (Hunger, whose gossamer, moth-like presence—a hovering of lacewings—quavers without brushing me, nearly a floating signifier we bless with our own meanings, or else a cloud winking in absentia.) Alas, these scripted imaginations are ontological thought experiences, and the ebb and tide of hunger does not depart from Yang's bodily aquarium of abstinence mixed with desire.

Of course, as a cloud, I have no flaming appetites or longings—neither hormonal drives nor wanton self-indulgence. (I am, dear reader, neither a subject of agony nor an object of desire, but simply a receptacle of data scripted to impart tales embedded in my cloudbank by millennial storytellers.) Once abuzz with information, now I glide afar from my clusters and servers. (And does this observation approach nostalgia or hunger? As a concept, nostalgia is a mode of knowing vis-à-vis absence, while hunger expresses an architecture of sensations intangible to me as happiness.)

✦

Menthol fumes of a eucalyptus log in Yang's fireplace lance the air with sinus-wakening vigor. (As a

dispossessed cloud, I have no sinuses but rather, a surfeit of synonyms and figures of speech, i.e. figments
of vicarious experience lived by Yang's poetry and by
proxy.) Yang extinguishes the smoldering wood with an
iron skillet, a griddle which he uses to fry buckwheat
dorayaki. For a minute, as the brilliant light of oranges
cascades into Yang's shanty, those blood-orange jewels
aglow in a cloud of unfiltered data. (If I wore a pen-
dulous garb of protoplasm, I'd bleed bits of data, those
nodes and petabytes triggering Yang's cloudy memories of running bare-legged through orange groves, as
Yang once did in boyhood. Where did those acres of
orange groves go after the rise of the mezzopolis?) The
callused palms of Yang's hands clap the smoky air while
I freewheel, a starry microcloud reduced to a ghost of
the panoply I once was. (Verily, I say, dear reader, I'm
a prolix one by all means, thanks to my gardener who
stashed his glossariums in me.) I cast no shadow. *Causa
latet, vis est notissima*, or a cause is hidden, but the result
is renowned.

✦

Every other moon, Yang looks forward to his walk to the
ragbag barter in the mezzopolis, especially for artisanal
honey. (In this new world order, you do not buy. You barter for honey of the monofloral kind, for instance, with a
kilogram of quinoa. Clover honey, acacia honey, mesquite
honey of the creosote desert, intoxicating red honey—
neurotoxin of rhododendrons in woven baskets lowered
off sheer, jagged rockface. Honey of the immune-boosting
manuka bush with a profusion of plum-colored blossoms.

Wound-healing bush jelly of a broom tea-tree, and one of Yang's favorites, honey-crystallized ginger root in shaved petals.) The denizens devised a way to save vanishing analog honeybees by simulating winter in diminished ultraviolet, an artificially induced hiberation, in turn promoting the longevity of bees corralled into bee ranches. By a suite of predictive formulae, however, the bees would eventually vanish in the great regression. Before the collapse, the mortality rate of bees would skyrocket regardless of aggressive bioreforms by the nine muses.

After the collapse, in an astonishing regeneration, the analog bees of exoskeletal gauze and sweet abdominal gold slowly returned. (Yang's garden would go barren without analog bees.) Even with the miracle of the bees, however, the denizens failed to recover even a mote of happiness of a remote ilk. For a microcloud with a silver lining, however, there's at least one sliver of a gainful margin. (The fervent valentines of the universe, slowing in blueshift light the color of bruised larkspur, fibrillate in the chasm between love and xenophobia. The mezzopolis is a lost sanctuary of sorts where mazuma no longer circulates, one where data analysts once dreamed of clairvoyant fiscal transactions in the form of cryptocurrency. A glittering rain of artificial intelligence—reedier than the silvery hairs of a centenarian, thinner than glassy threads of rice flour—never touches the ground, thanks to the lost clouds of the collapse.)

✦

After the failure of artificial rainfall in the biosphere, nothing grew. During the initial nights after the collapse, the denizens, plagued by hunger, realized they couldn't subsist solely on mung beans and other micro-greens doubling as pod insulation. (No more sweet corn, no bulgar wheat and pearled barley, no pseudocer-eal amaranth, no cherry orchards by storm lakes where Yang once swam with sleek, shining minnows as a boy. No blossoming orange and lemon groves survived to the west, and no more winter wheat to the north. No rhu-barb or blueberries, no fennel and rosemary flourishing by yesterday's squash and fava beans, no glossy auber-gines, no allium leeks.) The cloud-gardeners regretted the jargon of the junta, who uttered, *ecce panis angelo-rum*. Behold the bread of angels. What angels? What heavenly bread? Only the beclouded moon, blankly mirrored in a marshy fens, gazed at the mezzopolis. No cabbages, no chard, and no kohlrabi under rainfed clouds of yore—only the superblooming wildflowers and peat-grasses of fenland bogs. Famine. (Yet fauna and flora soon returned in a trophic cascade without the onslaught of alpha predators.)

In a standard albeit dead tongue of the empire: *alis grave nil,* or in an Anglophone translation, nothing is heavy with wings. Not even hunger. In another rendi-tion, nothing with wings is burdensome. (The angel of translation, interpreter of chiseled necropolises, once murmured in low-rolling fog—*invictus maneo*. I remain unvanquished.) Where is the botfree love that holds together the atoms of our existence?

If only we could slow down the light, savor each photon inscribed with love—every jot and tittle of light is a fervent valentine of the universe, pulsing at a rate slower than our irradiated hearts—each dance of light, a pas de deux slower than light itself.

＋

VALENTINES AT THE SPEED OF LIGHT

While passing through water or glass, light
slows, we already see. Skinless, every photon
slows to one velocity
                    in one pulse of light, a novelty—
as fervent valentines of the universe invisibly
limit the speed of photons in free space,
the rate at which slow light diminishes the gap
        between love and xenophobia.

Three | On Soul Conjectures

ON SOUL CONJECTURES

Can we save a soul in a jar—
And if not,
What anchors it to this life?
          Can we do surgery on a soul?
If so, then what is excised, and how?
     As for things we cannot see—
What does a soul hold?

✦

Even if Yang's quarantine is graced by the horticultural beauty of a sloping orchard under cloudfree skies, the denizens do not feel significantly happier after the collapse. A neo-rustic lifestyle, where a sack of pears is traded for a jar of kombucha is exchanged, in turn, for a string of fresh-caught mackerel, means our denizens must embrace a new level of proprioception. In other words, how do we thread our needles? What is our sense of where our body exists in space, a sensory aggregate of parts? How do we know where we are without our geographic positioning systems? How do we map out a massive, congestive network failure? Who are we? (Because

I am a cloud, I fail to understand the desires of these oddball bioforms and above all, their hypochondria and navel-gazing obsessions. And why do the living wish to livestream their lives, for instance?) How do we achieve happiness without the mood-adjusting cloudbits, those microdevices of biodata and biofeedback tailored by molecular design, gene on gene, nucleotide on nucleotide, to our genomes?

✦

Adroitly shuttling the jade beads on his abacus, Yang contemplates his private revelations with gratitude. Indeed, contrary to myths about alleged dataphobia and dysgraphia, the junta had gathered big, critical data identifying special denizens as catalysts for an antidote to dysthymia, i.e. the seven harbingers of happiness. The nine muses of the junta, in a pro bono spirit of benevolent governance, wished to override the raging blaze of analytics by minimization while revitalizing the imagination. *Poetae erit salvificem mundum.* Poets will save the world, not our manic pixie dreamclouds. (To resuscitate a lyric imagination, I whisper in his ear. And what is lyric, I say, in a song without words or vice versa? I don't know the Latin word for pixie, anyway.) As Yang already knows, the junta's campaigns—for wellness, for inspiration, for minimization—were launched to wipe out workaholism, monotony, opioids, greenhouse gases, and dysthymia—not necessarily in that order. Paradoxically, the junta aimed to do so by gathering big, critical data to maximize the common good while minimizing data overload. Along with dashboards, the junta added an elliptical poem alluding to a soul conjecture proved by a reclusive mathematician, as follows. (The proof demonstrates in the general case $K \geq 0$, Sharafutdinov's retraction $P : M \rightarrow S$ is a submersion.)

✦

Soul Conjecture. Suppose (M, g) is complete, connected and non-compact with sectional curvature $K \geq 0$, and there exists a point in M where the sectional curvature (in all sectional directions) is strictly positive.

    Then the soul of M is a point; equivalently M is diffeomorphic to R^n.

✦

ON SOUL CONJECTURES
AND DIFFEOMORPHISM

In this conjecture

        A topological surface

One without skin   *Boundaryless*

Where S is a soul

            A submanifold M in this case

A manifold resembles a Euclidean space x, y, z

    As a radius approaches zero

A circle, shrinking on a sphere, turns into a dot
In other words

Singularity

When time is a parameter

Suppose in conversing about the soul

What we know is limited to five senses

If anti-matter does not exist   Does a soul?

What proof demonstrates

What you propose?

If all three-dimensional objects
     are spheres

Can we keep the soul in a jar   And if not

What anchors it to this life?

Can we do surgery on a soul?

If so, then what is excised, and how?

Then the soul of M is a point. Equivalently

M is diffeomorphic to R^n

As for things we cannot see
What does a soul hold?

If the proof is correct—

No other recognition is needed.

✦

The junta's black bento box is inlaid with mother-of-
pearl tile, each one about the size of a koi fish-scale,
one square millimeter, an artifact of utility and beauty

harkening back to the technicians of antiquity before the common era. Yang opens the shiny lid to a bitter fragrance of herbal roots, but the box doesn't house medicine. Pausing to tousle his black-chestnut widow's peak and close his eyes, Yang broods over this metaphysical puzzle and its sequence of abstract questions and mathematical assertions. Is there such a thing as a soul proof, or vice versa, a proof of a soul? Does it pose inquiries about whether denizens of data can prove the existence of the soul? Is this an absurd question—a soul requires no proof by definition of faith? If a soul doesn't exist, then aren't we confined to empirical realities? If there is no afterlife, then is the biosphere only a pear-shaped blob of mud, and we are no more than our nervous dysthymia, star-crossed navel-gazing, and gastrointestinal peristalsis? (Speaking of which, Yang dips his face into a cloud of steam over a bowl of green sencha tea to clear his solar plexus and belly.)

+

Despite not scoring exceptionally well on a vocational assessment for beclouded happiness planners, Yang surmises, not wholly inaccurately, the keys to happiness probably include altruism (risk of ingratitude) as a matter of a civilized society, biodevices (risk of failure due to flaws in production or operational misuse) and quotidian inventions (risk of befuddlement) such as silicone drain hairgrippers (risk of spawning mildew, streptococcus, other toxic microbes) or genetically modified shampoo made without sodium lauryl sulfate (risk of neurotoxicity), tiny sky-blue trapezoids embossed with fine print in

3.0 font (risk of memory loss, fever, embolism, hyper-ventilation, increased appetite, weight gain, weight loss, eczema, hives, seizure, blindness, loss of night vision, decreased libido, hair growth in odd places, segmented sleep, insomnia, anxiety, nausea, tinnitus, hallucinations, somnambulism, gas and bloating, giddiness, and blue-colored pee), polymer splat balls squeezed for stress release (risk of rupture, leakage, and discoloration), all potential keys to unlocking happiness expressed in a polyglot quartet of global tongues—classical Latin (spy language everybody knows), Equatoguinean Spanish (most eloquent of tongues), Anglophone English (global tongue), and of course, Uberasian Mandarin (fiscal tongue).

In the wee hours of the night, after briskly toning his forehead with a hemp rag soaked in rosewater, Yang finishes his computations of the biometric, demographic, and geographical data points, identifying each one of the seven harbingers of happiness. Over a bowl of hot seaweed broth, Yang wonders whether it might be worthwhile to visit each denizen to see what could be gleaned for wisdom's sake—if not in designing a blueprint for a new world order, then at least to explore, more out of curiosity than virtue, whether systems of governance are malevolent in-and-of themselves, and whether those who hold power are inherently guilty. Are systems neutral instruments, regardless of methods? For instance, the junta was rumored to send exploding candy grams, lethal to its dissident recipients. The junta was criticized for censorship during the information wars, which nearly obliterated figurative language, even while they broadcasted, *poetae erit salvificem mundum*. Poets will save the world, revitalize a data-deluged populace supported by conscripted bots. Were the nine muses idealists who imagined a utopia of minimally invasive analytics on the one hand, or were they depraved despots of disinformation on the other? Did their clouded militia of happiness planners spin candy floss, or did they radicalize wellness in the fiefdoms? Neither a confectioner, didactic pedagogue, decolonial cartographer, dashboard superstar, pharmacologist, nor a biopolitician, Yang suspects it is none the above.

✦

To the boisterous noise of gossiping fisherman who can no longer use bots to transmit and analyze radar-doppler, and who therefore resort to forecasting weather based on analog clouds or the sky's color at sunset—red sky at night, sailors delight; red sky at morning, sailors take warning, and who wildly disagree with each other's predictions— Yang pinpoints, through the junta's suite of algorithms, the microbiography of an immunological prodigy, a little girl who has developed a cure for a lingering ailment of the post-collapse mezzopolis, namely, that ancient plague which launched a thousand sociocultural warships, the noxious contagion of xenophobia.

The girl's location matches the coordinates for the first harbinger of happiness decoded out of the black bento box. Her name in the Anglophone tongue is decoded as a single letter, A. In binary code, 01000001. In Mandarin it is the ideograph for peace, an. This word, in turn, is translated into Spanish as paz, and transliterated as Ana. Every detail in her biometric data—iris striations, earlobe geometry, fingerprints—suggests she is nine years old, including her birthday and year. Yang jots down her position and locality, plotted in Cartesian coordinates.

What does the first harbinger of happiness allegedly know about dispelling the fear or dislike of strangers? A case study in a nutshell, or rather, a sniffing bottle. The afflicted xenophobic subject uncorks a sniffing bottle, apparently, one like the nettle-extract tonic bottles of yore one may purchase at sensory integration boutiques, and inhales deeply. The xenophobic antigens—or more accurately, antigens of xenophobia—are rendered useless by the immunoglobulin. Is it too good to be true? His mother used to say, *bīng dòng sān chǐ fēi yī rì zhī hán*. Three feet of cold ice is not the result of one cold day.

Setting off with a burlap satchel of mochi and a bamboo thermos of matcha tea, Yang emerges from his self-imposed quarantine by the sea. It sparkles turquoise before his eyes, white-capped with the westerly winds, and intensifies to cyan (wavelengths green to blue), aqua, phtalo, ultramarine, violet, and indigo (wavelengths 425 to 250 nanometers). He travels four nights by fishing boat on the coast, immersed in the salty chatter of the fishermen on the waves, then walks four and three-quarter hours on foot in the mezzopolis where a multimedia miasma once blurred the tranquillized noggins of its denizens.

+

At the top of nine floors of sleeping-pods bedecked with a zig-zagging fire escape, one of those pseudonymized

turrets of the mezzopolis, the nine-year old immunological prodigy, whose solemn eyes settle on Yang with the
color of charlotte russe, resides with her widowed mother.
Her father, Yang learns, was a casualty of cyberfatigue during the information wars. Perched on the edge of a rattan
chair, Ana sits on little round fists while her mother carries
a tray of ginger-flavored orange pekoe tea to the folding
coffee table.

After proffering his gift of mochi stuffed with azuki
red-bean paste, Yang pours a cup of tea out of a pot-infuser
of tempered glass, then drops in a stick of cinnamon bark.
Crowded with lush greenery, the penthouse pod with a
sunroof offers hydroponically grown lettuce, alfalfa and
chia, feathergrass, air-filtering fronds of tillandsia, and
borosilicate flasks festooned with blue-green spirulina.
Modest in total square footage (544 sq. ft.), the pod's spa-
tial arrangement maximizes every inch of utility, including
natural light. Ana, please tell me, Yang begins. I hear that
you're an immunological prodigy. How did you discover
that xenophobia is an antigen, not a behavior or disposi-
tion shaped by negative social forces?

When my great-great grandma crossed the great-
great river to migrate north, she carried a secret recipe inside a flask. No, wait a minute. It was my great-great-great
grandma, not great-great. Right, mama? (Her mother
nods.) It's a recipe we passed down for generations, along
with our humility salve for affluenza. You open the jar, take
a whiff. Affluenza, silver-spoons-in-mouth syndrome, or
squid-like languor due to growing up with tons of mazuma, gone. It reeks, though. You have to rub it on your face,
throat, and chest. It fights vanity, egotism, and narcissism
better than nucleoside analogues and antiretrovirals. One
of the active ingredients is a drop of immunotherapeutic

water from the bayou, and the bulk of it is an extract of raw, pureed durian, 1-sulfanyl-ethanethil, a skunky decoction. Have you ever tasted durian, mister? (Yang nods.) When you crack it open, it looks like vanilla cream pudding but stinks to the hereafter. When I was seven, I isolated this compound. I loved working in my own virtual lab, which my dad built in the portal when we lived in a bigger pod before he died of massive data overload.

You loved your papa very much, Ana.

When papa was alive, I also correctly identified the antigen, xenophobia. It's an immunoglobulin which neutralizes the xenophobic antigen. I was pod-schooled by my parents before the commonwealth revamped it with outcomes-only assessments.

Pod-schooling is marvelous.

When I took the vocational assessment, I tested as a competency-qualified pharmacologist at age seven, but I was too young to work. So my parents and I designed my own cloud to help me fulfill my calling as a pharmacologist.

What type of cloud, Ana?

Before the bad data killed him, my papa worked as a virtual reality manager. He especially loved helping clients livestream their daily lives in the mezzopolis so others could live vicariously and perform better on their assessments. For example, I always wanted to be a pharmacologist when I grew up. According to the vocational assessment, I was already a pharmacologist, but I couldn't work because I was only seven. Mister, let me tell you. This was so depressing. My mama says that I started exhibiting symptoms of dysthymia. I was glued to mood-calibrating clouds, sat on and broke my ultralight gourd-lute which papa carved out of a genetically modified calabash, and cried almost all the time. Because I lived inside clouds, I scored in the lowest zone of a sensory processing assessment. That's when my papa designed the gourd-lute, so I could learn to process sensory information by plucking monochords and humming. I wasn't very good, as my genome is missing the key sequences for harmony, pitch, and rhythm genes. I accidentally sat on the gourd-lute. Boom. After I broke it, my parents signed me up for alternative dreamcloud therapy to get those repetitive negative thoughts adjusted.

Did it help?

Cloud after cloud, more of the same cloudscape. Garbage in, garbage out. Finally, my papa designed a cloudbased pharmacy simulation with fake medicines for virtual clients and my very own clinical research pods and information banks, where I could input data. Not analog, mind you, mister. Papa engineered my very own cloud, the most amazing cloud ever. He edited bioinformatics harvested from the livestreams of grown-up pharmacologists, then stored them in my cloud. Now, after the collapse, we barely do anything. We have no clouds to amuse, edify, or inform us. We can't go anywhere without consulting a paper map. We're forced to use our imaginations, for crying out loud. We can't use opioids because they're bad, anyway. So what do we do? We doodle algorithms and flowcharts in our heads, but who cares. No one wishes to do long division by hand. We drink tea and talk. My mama says this is actually a better way of living, wholesome like the predigerati of years ago who dialogued face-to-face outside clouds.

It can't all be so bad.

I do like growing our own heirloom squash in a commune of nine stacked pods, and we use the squash to barter for eggs, safflower oil, and amaranth flour so we can bake a gluten-free version of pudding cake over a stove biofueled by sterilized fruitbat guano. The kabocha pumpkin and bonbon winter squash are the best ones.

Could you please say more about this antigen?

It's humanity attacking itself.

What do you mean, Ana?

Us, as a species, turning against ourselves.

Ana, the disorder you've described, an autoimmune syndrome, suggests a physiological condition, namely—an immune system attacking its own tissues. Aren't these two strikingly different phenomena? One is bodily in origin, and the other is not. For example, before the rise of information, predigerati falsely believed that race was a biologically predetermined trait. Are we back to measuring skulls and frontal cortex size, all that ridiculous nonsense? The value systems we attach to ourselves are social constructs of faulty logic and implicit bias in power structures used to subjugate and exploit others. Could you please explain how xenophobia is no different than an immunodeficiency or a gluten allergy like celiac disease?

That's like refusing to believe in penicillin, the atom, or the alpha and omega.

Her mother's contralto voice rises, a tonal shift in the conversation. Ana, please remember to show our guest how the immunoglobulin works. And please ask him if he'd like more tea. After the collapse, we don't have many guests visiting our pod from the other side of the mezzopolis, and Mister Yang walked a long way to come and see us. Mister Yang even brought us homemade mochi with azuki, one of your favorites.

How did you know, Mister Yang?

A little bird told me.

Which bird?

It's a figure of speech, Ana.

Quietly, the prodigy uncaps a glass sniffing bottle in the shape of a little amphora with fiddlehead handles. Instantly, the potent fragrance of a moveable dessert feast—first, with the piquancy of crystallized ginger, then chocolate-robed raspberries atop scoops of hazelnut gelato juxtaposed to a buttery wheel of apricot-studded brie-en-croute, an oozing blackberry cobbler garnished with sweet whipped cream, a buttery summer peach pie with a crumb topping and crème fraîche, a sour cream bundt cake with a zesty lemonade drizzle, glazed pistachio tartlets, even his mother's black forest gateaux and trays of almond cookies, and a chocolate mousse torte with demitasses of espresso—wafts into the pod, filling Yang's olfactory senses with a flowering abundance of a million cocoa tea-roses distilled in copper florentines. Miraculously, hate vaporizes for a nano-second. Xenophobia—whether misprogrammed neural activity, learned negative behaviors, or antigens—evaporate at a whiff. Only love holds together the atoms of the universe, wherein one would lay down one's life for another, a sacrifice only available in a prodigy who heeds the invisible angels of invention and their divine engines of hallelujahs.

Maybe the bread of angels does exist, says Yang.

The girl looks questioningly into Yang's face.

May I take a few of these bottles with me?

Ana glances at her mother, who shakes her head. God created everything for a purpose, even the old bayou of ancestral bones and alligator's teeth. As one of the modern saints of the second millennium once said, *We ourselves feel that what we are doing is just a drop in the ocean. But the ocean would be less because of that missing drop.* Nothing under heaven, in all of God's creation, could be given in exchange for this antidote, not even the greatest-greats and greater-than-greats dredged up from the bayou.

Doesn't love function as a paradox?

What do you mean, mister?

More of it exists if you give it away.

Ana, with a shy smile, slips a vial into Yang's open hand, where it burns like a kindling flame from a hearth of happiness in his boyhood.

✦

As Yang walks down the zig-zag stairs inside the turret of sleeping-pods, a ballooning shadow of night—ominously, a throwback to the empire's gigantic fiscal bubble before it burst—looms over the fizzled mezzopolis. The docking stations of a smog-eating cybrary lie dormant under the skywalk, the data warehouses of star and snowflake schema obscured by sea fog. The analog flying foxes of the air, the fruitbats with the wingspan of a child, roost under the eaves and orifices of the rotunda, upside-down like furled umbrellas in the groove of a coat rack or a lacquered tree. In this stratospheric state of dysthymia, will our denizens bridge the far distance between love and xenophobia, more than a stone's throw away? Or will the abyss dividing strangers and lovers endure in the gloom of yesterday's smoky data-dens?

At this juncture, dear reader, you can judge me as a frivolous cloud with a veneer of sentimentalism unanchored in scientific inquiry. Rather, I'm not as amorphous as one might assume, recessed in a finitude of psychometrics stored by adept gardeners whose ciphertexts and hairline cursors once projected analytics on massive jumbotrons captioned in every other tongue. Consider me a blighted neo-romantic at best, a cloud with an inclination

67

for the empirical. While the corpulent basin of your soul glides on a fleshy aquarium of information—a brain, a gray chrysanthemum, three-quarters water, a fatty system of axons and dendrites firing together, an encephalous maze of clouded, myelin-sheathed impulses—I possess no such marvelous organ. As a microcloud, I have no flaming appetites, either—no hormonal drives, no false wishes. (I am, dear reader, neither a subject of agony nor an object of desire, but a receptacle of data scripted with a tale.)

DEAR MILLENNIUM, LOVE

Before I fell asleep last night, a double-star conjunction
shone so blindly, I fished it out of the west

with a rag of spider silk lost by the woolly bold jumper.
Please fix my bandwidth
           so I do more sensible things.

Young skyscrapers, after falling, are going up, jagged
           scapes in a nanosecond,

scaffolded and reconstructed in smoke. Millennium
of burned, hairless marigolds,
           of cataclysmic seaquakes, grenades

and dazzling insects not lasting the night: grant ourselves
permission for intimacy, for freedom to choose

whom we love while on earth
           even if we do not love whom we ought.

✦

Four | The Angel of the Future

THE ANGEL OF THE FUTURE

Wearing the longest, brightest sleeve over heaven
and the divested mezzopolis, the angel of the future
is less of a prophet for our post-collapse existence
than a messenger of hope from the ancient days—
unlike the quandary of those who cannot see
　　　　　the future waiting in dark hours
and days ahead—say, one disinterested in living
yet who doesn't quite wish to die, either—
the angel's written on his sleeve: dear exile,
　　　　　post-digital apocalypse—
　　　　　　　　dum spiro spero,
　　　　　　　　　while I breathe, I hope.

✦

Yang circles back to his seaside shanty with a drop of
the bayou in his dungarees, sealed in a brass-capped
bottle reminiscent of Chinese snuff bottles displayed
at the sensory processing, detoxifying boutique below
the dodecahedral, wind-powered pod where he resided
prior to the collapse. As a boy, Yang loved examining
the miniature bottles of jade, quartz, or agate exquisitely

hand-painted by Qing artisans predating Uberasia by a millennium, once appraised at forty thousand dollars per set in the days of affluenza. Look, but don't touch, his mother would say, holding his little hands, which he'd flex in futile protest. (He isn't a fan of snuff itself, however, outlawed by the nine muses alongside fossil fuels and ultraviolet sunshine salons, an embargo which contributed, in Yang's analysis, to the collapse.)

⁺

How to shrink the dysthymic void between our hearts, expand the radius of love?

⁺

With huzzahs of glee, Yang hops into the sea air, clicks the soles of his zori flipflops, the antidote to xenophobia stowed away in the kangaroo pocket of his dungarees. Lifting his quill pen—a goose feather-shaft scoured clean of barbs—dipped briskly in sepia ink, he outlines a rough blueprint for the mechanical reproduction of the anti-xenophobic immunoglobulin in artisanal, hand-crafted quantities. If only he could put his hands on industrial-size fragrance atomizers to puff clouds of airborne immunoglobulin into the biosphere, the post-collapse mezzopolis might be delivered of xenophobia altogether in one delicious squirt of the bayou—alligator teeth, muskrat bones, and all. (Yang seldom misses the days when he was a vigilante who relished the crisp skin of sitting ducks exposed in ponzi schemes without a twinge of guilty conscience. I am a reformed man in this era, he writes in his gardening journal. The daikon radish is maturing in cool weather, and soon I'll make daikon pickle.)

✦

What is the fragrance of love in a dystopic universe?

✦

The nine-muse junta, according to vestiges of rumorville in the darkling twilight of data leading to the eve of the fiscodigital collapse, also worried about suicide rates in the fiefdoms of data. Did a surfeit of data trigger paralysis in face of decision-making? (The answer is yes.) Did a profusion of facts and figures reinforce a sense of alienation, especially in the mezzopolis where nocturnal guests in a microhotel of sleeping-pods snoozed only inches away from a stranger's nostrils, dazed by a world-weary cloud of worthlessness? Of data-induced paralysis exacerbated by a virulent strain of renegade scripts? Cloud on cloud, where did one denizen begin, and another end? The nine muses of the junta—postmodern herstory, synthetic music, astrophysics or radioastronomy, love and comedy in stereo as romantic comedy, epic poetry slam, electrochoreography, post-traumatic memory, and domestic tragedy of the ages—thickened their data by conducting brisk interviews with focus groups in addition to slicing and dicing a morass of demographics.

On a swatch of palm husk, Yang scribbles the next decrypted binary code in the black bento box, which yields a name and geographic coordinates. The precise locality is identified by latitude and longitude.

+

With a gift of angel food cakes riding in his satchel, Yang hitches a ride on the briny deck of a krill-and-langostino boat which harvests more analog jellyfish than either krill or langostino, huffing its slow way to an isle off the coast. Thanks to global warming, the jellyfish migrated through currents (85 degrees Fahrenheit, 30.44 degrees Celsius) and multiplied fruitfully along the coast, rising and falling with the global oscillation in the biosphere. To the fishermen's dismay, the ocean teems with their frilled, gelatinous bells and stinging aquatresses. *A trash fish*, said one fisherman, *like sting rays, skates, and electric eels. No one will exchange anything for trash fish*. In two tongues—Mandarin and the Anglophone tongue—Yang explains how one man's trash is another man's delicacy, and how to prepare lightly scalded jellyfish with miso, scallions, and soy sauce. Briskly slice the flesh in ribbons, he says, motioning on a diagonal. Like a julienned zucchini but in longer ribbons, like this. (I still recall the other jellyfish of biodata, dear reader, which used a high bandwidth prior to congestive network failure.)

Out to sea, Yang gulps the iodine-flavored air and salt spray of the choppy waves. He sports a pair of hand-knitted acupressure bracelets over the P6 Neiguan points on each wrist to abate motion sickness. Hard to believe that the sea, before the collapse, was the world's largest data dump. When he was a boy, his mother and father would take him to the ocean for sandwich picnics on the beach before it was polluted by disinformation. (This is analog sand, his actuarial father would explain, running his fingers on the ground, versus a sandwich, named after an earl who lived eons ago, not a data sandbox. Little Yang would protest, dubiously, the notion of eating any type of sand, figurative or not.) Then his mother and father would take him to the lake for the summer, where he jumped off a floating dock and swam with minnows. Why does he recall those years with dim nostalgia? Nebulous clouds of mystery, so bittersweet to parse, and tougher to filter than 350 million trillion liters of bad data in the seven seas. (The first movement on the surface of his dreams, journeying back in time to his boyhood, is the beaming face of his silvering grandmother as she told stories of the mythical peach boy who saved his village from wolves. Or was it bandits?) Yang disembarks from the boat, waves farewell to the fishermen, and walks onto the jetty into the mute speedways of the mezzopolis.

+

Who is the angel of the future?

To all appearances nondescript, a middle-aged man waits on a plexiglass bridge, watching for jumpers. Blowing his nose in a wad of biodegradable cellulose pulped from analog rope, the man says, I apologize for my sinuses. Working on this skywalk has inflamed my respiratory system, and now it's hypersensitive to fruitbat guano. In the midst of a bat plague, I was attacked by those rabid flying foxes, who bit my face and inoculated me with bat saliva, then pooped on my head. A boil erupted. I took a nasty assortment of herbal antibiotics, which in turn damaged my digestive tract.

Yang offers the gift of cakes.

The man accepts the gift with a bow. With genuine apologies, I'm also severely allergic to egg albumen. I break out in hives inside my throat. Angioedema, it's called. Please forgive my poor introduction. I am not usually so negative, my friend. I save the despondent from committing suicide by hauling each survivor back onto the skywalk in a bear hug, or better yet, persuading each one not to jump at all, says the man who is nicknamed the angel of the future. My aim is to save an entire skywalk of denizens from leaping to their deaths. The skywalk—he gestures east to west—was constructed during the information wars. The lookout would warn snipers that the foe was coming, a method of surveillance which proved risky for the lookout as well as for the snipers, even in the days of the digerati's hegemony controlled by bots from the alcoves of multiversities.

What was your livelihood before this? asks Yang.

I served in the junta's great leap sideways to stamp out workaholism during the wide-sweeping minimization reforms implemented by the junta. During the great leap for the common good, when we were exhorted to love our neighbors at least as much as our own navels, my father used to serve as a factory worker before the regime provided white collar jobs for everyone within five points of a vocational assessment with a supplementary intelligence quotient tool. Those who scored below a certain proficiency benchmark were placed on a five-year subsidized plan to work in the analog factories—tapping the pitted caps of thimbles for quality control, checking the bevel and groove of polycarbonate sunglasses, and so forth before the automated workforce replaced everybody who could fog a spoon, as my father put it, jokingly. My father preferred the esprit de corps of factory work over the white-collar desk job as a certified tax collector for the outlying territories, one who collected a post-byzantine tax on hearthstones, and he often lamented scoring so high on the assessment. A son of Anglophone migrants with predigerati origins, my father idealized factory work, failing to recognize how those workers were treated as inferior to automatons, divorced from their artisanal craft and relegated to apparatuses in the greased axles of capitalism. At least the automatons got their solar cells upgraded from time to time, and didn't actually feel the pain of burnout when their cartridges exploded. The factory workers were sort of human precursors to the bots.

What do you think of this bridge?

This skywalk is a stunning work of art wedded to utility and pragmatism. You can view the mezzopolis under it, the cloudfree learning commons, and drained beds on the landfilled shoreline where data dumps used to fester. However, despite its splendor, it is a bridge of heaven or hell. For those who cross it to go spearfishing for pleasure or to trade provisions at the flea market, for those who swim to it as fugitives, or those caretakers who buff it with chamois from sunup until sundown, it could be a road of promise. For those who try to jump, on the other hand, it is a different tale altogether.

Did you save anyone yesterday?

Yesterday was a slow day on the skywalk. No one crossed my watch. However, the day prior, I hauled a girl of sad eyebrows back onto the bridge. She was dangling one leg over the side when I spotted her with my binoculars. As I listened to her story, I realized that she was utterly despondent about her powerlessness to see into the light of the ensuing day. Figuratively, I mean. Over a hot bowl of scallion broth, her shoulders wrapped in a makeshift rain-coat—one I improvised from knotting together my tissues while a cloud of rainy mist glided over us—she told me that absolutely nothing and nobody awaited her in a living pod left by her deceased parents, who found no purpose beyond caring for their only daughter. When she left to study tele-cloud tinkering at the multiversity, her mother and father were plagued by empty nest syndrome and found no reason to live, either. Thinner than the milky afternoon light pass-ing through her skin while she shivered like a willow leaf on the bridge, she'd fought my life-saving bear hug on the sky-walk with every bloody tooth and nail, as the saying goes. Please forgive the mixed metaphors. Willow, bear, tooth, I mean. Banned during the information wars. And to envi-sion herself in the future, or try seeing a future at all, was no less than death. And I should mention, if you don't mind, this girl of sad eyebrows was exquisitely beautiful. I do not mean this in a humdrum sense. I do not intend to senti-mentalize melancholy. Mesmerizingly otherworldly, not of this place, sad eyebrows and tissues and all.

Do you know where she is now?

No.

Do you sense that she's alive?

I don't know.

Doesn't it bother you?

Let us be content to abide in uncertainties, sir.

Why else do people try to jump?

Where does the future go when you can't see it any-more? (The man unwraps an angel cake, sniffs cautiously, sneezes, and nods appreciatively. This is good. Marvelous fragrance, he says. Amaretto extract. Food of the angels, indeed. Let's say I partake vicariously of your tasty gift through the power of my creative imagination.) During

the great leap sideways to reduce cyberfatigue, our livelihood ironically consisted of dashboarding, day and night,
the impact of those regulations, old and new, on outcomes
defined by the common good, i.e. restoring the imagination, revitalizing our vitality, et cetera. However, it was a
hoax. Everyone knew the oligarchical order of polity no
longer existed under the junta. Goes without saying, the
majority of the new regulations were absurd, and no angels of information carried reams of analytics to us each
morning, so it was all garbage in, garbage out. The junta
disposed of the oligarchy by sprinkling smart dust on their
jump seats in the parliament, a mock assembly. Although
the dust was harmless, the oligarchy thought it was rice
powder contaminated by arsenic from toxic rice paddies.
Their psychosomatic deaths were due to shock. The smart
dust, rather, was engineered for gathering intelligence in
the spy language everybody knew, Latin.

Astonishing. I didn't hear about the smart dust.

Maybe it was ricin, although I doubt it. Even if the
papillomavirus was eradicated through advances in eco-
feminist biotechnology, and despite our use of nitrogen-
rich fruitbat guano as a biofuel—the fiscal equivalent of
flax spun into gold—dysthymia still paralyzes the souls
of our denizens, even to this day of relative post-digital
liberty. I say, are we truly cloudfree? What is free will, if
such a thing exists, if a will is a thing? If I bite into a scallion dumpling in seaweed broth, does this choice mean
I'm free, or am I controlled by my carnal appetite? Did
clouds of big, critical data control our choices, or did we
control the clouds? Through our revitalizing, life-giving
actions, we show our good belief that hope exists for a
better future, even if it's simply about eating a handful of
strawberries or isolating a gene sequence for dancing the

zumba with extraordinary pizzazz.

In the new barter-exchange economy, bankruptcy is abolished, right?

No. In the past week, here are the reasons why denizens tried to end their lives. Craved a tube of nicotine vapor, yet none found. Chronic, intractable gastrointestinal dystopia. Dyspepsia, I mean. Depleted a stash of opioids. Or nasal corticosteroids. Ran out of algal caffeine. Kicked out of the house due to a spouse's discovery of photographs, shot using analog instant-roll film, of a romantic liaison prior to one's current marriage, along with a box of old-fashioned, handwritten letters in longhand. The failure of marriages arranged solely by compatability algorithms, and no muse of domestic tragedy showed up to narrate a new script. Falling I-beam. Attacked by fleas at the flea market. Excessive consumption of gluten. Anxiety. Jitters without chatbots to fill the void with sociable noise. Withdrawal symptoms from cloudbit addiction. Microdevice dependency. Vertigo of unknown cause. Very bad case of acne. Fear of a second fiscodigital apocalypse. Fear of analog spiders. An existential sinkhole of cloudfree living. Nausea to the point of no return, one man told me.

What do you do after you stop them from jumping?

I walk each one to my pod. We drink tea. I listen.

You listen?

The sad thing is, after hours of listening, I often agree, maybe you're right, your life isn't worth living. I mean, if you see no future outside commodities amassed prior to the fiscodigital collapse, or if your spouse refuses to go to counseling through a telecloud simulcast a stone's throw away from your zippered sleeping-pods, or you believe one of your hundred half-siblings who texts you from a pseudonymized egg bank where she vows to blackmail you about your mother's bioengineered gestational carrier, why bother? If you cannot exist without the chatter of bots asking you about the weather, and if the day holds too much suffering, and if your brain cannot withstand the ache of post-digital nausea or the heartbreak of not knowing your parents, why not just put it to rest? I can treat eczema with a salve of shea butter, aloe hydrogel, and eucalyptus oil. I can't fix a broken heart with triple-distilled seawater or heal a crumbling marriage with juniper berry tea. Even if we live in a post-mazuma, agrarian fiefdom now, I cannot promise the restoration of yesterday's affluenza or tomorrow's promise of agronomic abundance. In a mezzopolis of pervasive neurasthenia, where denizens feel too sad to get out of bed, I can only listen.

Because one hopes for the better, right?

So, I invite each one to serve alongside me on the bridge.

Why do you still work alone, then?

Nagging fear of the junta lingers—of their intelligence-scavenging omnipresence, their ceaselessly scanning eyes of merciless scrutiny and surveillance. Prior to the collapse, the junta supported this solo endeavor of mine, ironically. Indeed, before the empirical oligarchy—I refuse to refer to it as a commonwealth, as no wealth was truly shared in common—devolved into territorial fiefdoms. The oligarchy ran out of space in the necropolis, and crematories hosted interminable waiting lists. As you know, by the time the living rose to the top of the waiting list, they would be dead, so in an ironical way, this worked out. Utilitarian, yes, but the junta's puppets of benevolent despotism—or despotic benevolence, rather—chose to save lives rather than figure out what to do with cataloguing, stowing, and performing autopsies with biometric assessments on a million corpses, a sprawling nation-state of the dead. However, against their own policies of minimization, the junta wrote bylaws excommunicating those who interfered with suicide when overpopulation outpaced natural energy renewal, a problem deemed more serious than the interminable waiting lists at the crematories. And vigilantes of the junta could always perform burials at sea or launch the deceased into outer space—your loved ones among the starfish or the stars, if ash-to-ash wasn't a viable route, yet only a few chose these alternative methods of *memento mori*. I say, *ad astra per aspera*, or to the stars via adversity, the junta's motto.

Absurd. Why not chew raw ginger for nausea or take serotonin reuptake inhibitors?

Boredom doesn't actually kill, nor nausea by proxy, nor even despair. What I believe ultimately kills our denizens is a lack of vision for the future, a missing goal or purpose to fulfill, a loss of hope-infused dreams—by avocation, by divine calling, by engaging in a grand design bigger than ourselves—or a soul's unrealized architecture of desire. Or else the despondent are spoiled by instant gratification. Too much navel-gazing, too many silver spoons in the mouth. When life throws lemons at us, we analyze data about making lemonade. A cliché of a bygone age, no? Ounces of citric acid sealed in a waxy yellow rind? We overthink our figures of speech. Yet this lemonade principle is a foreign concept to this generation. No medicine exists for an epidemic of sour narcissism with neurasthenia riding upon its hairy back. No dosage of kava kava root, no mood-soothing tonics laced with norepinephrine, not even a tablespoon of hot almond milk with a drop of antimicrobial honey for ulcers, nor a shot of caffeinated chlorophyll can dispel melancholy for long.

What do you mean by neurasthenia?
You don't know?
Nervousness or neurosis?
A soul in exile.

✦

DEAR EXILE, DUM SPIRO, SPERO

We breathe, we hope, say the souls vested to survive
fire-bombings, night raids, annihilations of love.
Whom shall we trust, what camaraderie exists?
Truth or dare. No one designs beauty here; desire
nothing. War is no lovely thing, not a curative.
Truth, a girl once said to me, your body is made
to heal alone. Algal fog rolling every noon is no
remedy for nostalgia. No, this is not a pleasure—
nothing is holy in this world. Dare we inhabit
the post-human, a fractal ebb and flow of lymph
and laser? Bless our given bodies without reprisal
or regret. Borders we crossed as youth, invisible
at a distance when the fog lifts, no longer home.
Toxic compass rose of exile, carcinogenic blooms.
Skywalk under our soles exudes a bluing perfume,
notes of a failed paradise, of undocumented flight
from zone to sanctuary, exiles fleeing to the allure
of citizenry drawn by sea, by flood, by fire.

Five | The Water Doctor

THE WATER DOCTOR

A forecasting barometer of hand-blown glass,
a tidal moon—digital simulation of zebrafish
on zylonite,
        kettle-stitch
                deckle-edged sea wave,
    drum-leaf tender,
glassine
             wild-caught fish-bones
                or flyleaf isinglass—
Soon, says the water doctor,
in this volume
            of apocalyptic meteorology—
we'll be dropped in a rain squall
of data-deluged seas—
                    codex of ocean.

✦

Mending his zori flipflops with yellowed scraps of genetically modified fish skin fabricated prior to the collapse, Yang adjusts his visor and looks to the sun rising

in the east as his analog compass. The third harbinger of happiness, a water doctor, is tougher to find than the immunological prodigy and the angel of the future. A figurative needle in the hay, reflects Yang, contemplating the long journey of dead metaphors to a savannah biome of feathergrass, afflicted by famine and global warming, far beyond the phishing fiefdoms of poisoned waters when the fuliginous tide turned foul for months with bots pouring garbage analytics in, garbage out.

Yang inserts a chopstick in the ground and drops a stone at the end of its thin shadow. He waits ten minutes, then drops a second stone to the shadow's new position. With the chopstick, he draws a line in the dirt between the two stones, east to west. (This is opposite the direction he must follow, west to east; he makes a note on a fragment of dry palm husk with his goose-quill pen.)

+

Yang packs a fat clingstone peach, a sleeve of dehydrated jackfruit known as jackfruit leather, a water microfilter, and a dozen bamboo cylinders. According to the black bento box's suite of algorithms, Yang knows that it'd take at least two days on foot to reach the man's village if he used the thermobarically bombed-out speedways of the junta, past the beleaguered fields where those veiled-and-wimpled flying muses allegedly held their drumhead court-martial hearings to quash the dissidents.

+

During his expedition from the outskirts of the ruined mezzopolis, Yang observes the flourishing of flora and fauna, post-collapse: a shoeblack-eye of hibiscus and raised beds of woody roselles with bottle-brush trees, avocado pots with hermaphrodite flowers—female the first day, male the second day—in a feat of self-pollination like autogamous orchids (within a single flower rather than a tree), against the backdrop of concourses sealed as mausoleums to an underworld of the dead, a mute skyline of ports bereft of sizzling streams of real-time analytics. No droning fleets of low-coptering optical eyes. No fiscal balloons. No phishing or scamming fraudsters. As his mother would've said, *rén wú qiān rì hǎo, huā wú bǎi rì hóng*. No one has a thousand good days in a row, and no flower stays red for a hundred days. Nonetheless, a marshy river of effluvia flows through the mezzopolis to the sea, where it carries the blossoming flesh of those who could not live without their fiscodigitalia.

The way is winding, narrow, and monotonous under a blasting sun, but Yang is resolute about reaching his destination. After forty-eight hours of a grueling journey on foot, and eleven bamboo cylinders of microfiltered water later, Yang reaches a village of reed-thatched pods set in a circle with a radius of 17.4 yards. A bespectacled, bald man—on his nose, a lightweight pair of photosensitive glasses manufactured prior to the fiscodigital collapse—emerges from one of the pods. He sports a buttoned silk shirt and khakis with jute-rope sandals, evoking the humble mien of an anthropologist in the field—a stranger among strangers.

In the spirit of a gift economy, the two men engage in a glad exchange with good tidings—pressed cakes of dried figs for Yang's sleeve of jackfruit leather, and news of other hamlets in the fiefdoms, those recovering slowly from dysthymia, and others deceased or missing in Yang's remote fishing village. (Alas, no *new* news. No one knows much due to the lack of connectivity.)

+

The water doctor—his moniker on the clandestine, underground resistance against the junta—doesn't dwell in a gorgeous penthouse pod. No, the doctor doesn't live in a renovated cell turret near the seaside portals, or next to a delicatessen of thinly sliced, dry-cured imitation prosciutto translucent as the sea coral from which it was fabricated, or puffed rice curls in the shapes of seahorses, sprayed lightly with liquid smoke. Mezzanines of double-height pyrex ceilings and graceful, ornamental waterfalls are phenomena of yesteryear, a gilded age. He does not reside near the bougainvillea conservancy on the way to the virtual pet clinic for digital chinchillas of slight attention deficiency due to impaired dopamine modulation. Rather, he lives in a humble pod built with his own hands.

Before the collapse, the bespectacled doctor bought a hundred acres of drought-stricken desert on the outskirts of the mezzopolis. He vowed to use his knowledge to build a massive bowl in the ground for catching rainwater. Eighty acres wide, the huge bowl is lined with sand, barren soil, and pea gravel. (The retired doctor bore seven wells into the ground despite the firewheels of brush and tumbleweed igniting the candelabra trees and elephant grass in the drought, trailing the season of network outages.) Dwelling in a pseudonymized pod among pods, he feeds guinea fowl out of his own hands. The free-range guinea fowl relish plentiful crickets, flies, and honey locusts. The water doctor explains that he has found the guinea fowl are most effective at eliminating pesky insects in his yard, even more so than chickens, and the guineas are less inclined to scratch up his pea gravel for grubs.

Why not catch rainfall during the wet months for water during the summer?

The water doctor speaks in a clipped manner with an oblique chiasmus, mirroring his squarish hands in a cross-over gesture for emphasis. We do, my friend, although the biome's rainfall is unreliable in the late months of the year, due to an unpredictable polar jet stream. (The water doctor squints up at the sky, clouded by mist.) This is neither about storehousing liquid data nor liquid analytics, not even the formulae of fluid dynamics. We are stewards of hydrogen dioxide, the water that God has furnished in this earth and the vault of our sky. So, as a grassroots collective of water healers, we opened up the vessels of the heavenlies and unsealed the underground aquifers. Aqua vitae, the analog water of life beyond systems and infrastructures. Our hands bless the wellsprings, and the wellsprings bless our hands. My sons and daughters and their children's children will not go thirsty. Instead, we quench the thirst of the land, so the land may quench our thirst.

And you have no slush funds?

Nothing, my friend. We pray for water healers to answer the call. Healers, mind you, engage the miraculous beyond tangible works. And the junta, you know, promised us the figurative moon yet provided nothing; staunchly utilitarian and egalitarian in the dogma of minimizing overload, yet not pragmatic enough in translating their aspirations into praxis. In short, the exalted junta were no less than obnoxious, self-serving bureaucrats. We cannot depend on quixotic, wide-sweeping policy reforms on one hand, or intrinsically motivated altruism on the other. Nature is subject to the human, and the human is subject to nature. If it were not for this water bowl, fatalities would've risen due to a drought during the outages. We pray for the water healers, so they come, one by one. Women, fathers, mothers, girls and boys walking hand in hand like angels out of nowhere. Whole families, generations, the decades spawning their descendents, et cetera. After the collapse, we labor in the greenhouses of recycled windshields, trim our alfalfa-turf pods of homegrown insulation, weave homespun dresses of reclaimed polyester, and work to revitalize our mezzopolis of blood and non-blood kindred. We're a family-run cooperative of water healers, not an army of post-civilization's avengers, even though we combat drought and famine together.

Everybody's blood-related in Uberasia.

Yes. However, we're kindred not only because of the ubiquity of egg banks or our mitochondrial maternal ancestry traceable to one woman named Eve eons before the common era. Although we're 99.9 percent identical genetically, 2 to 3 million differences exist between my genetic fingerprint and yours. Family is a system of learned behaviors, not only blood, guts, and genes.

Why do people come?

No blood exists without water, and no water without blood.

What did you think of the junta?

The water doctor takes off his photosensitive glasses and polishes them with a swatch of unbleached cotton, the sweet hue of raw cane sugar. He puts them back on his face and squints at Yang, answering carefully, then crosses his hands for emphasis. Those who wish to fight corruption may find corruption is only fought within. Those who have good intentions to resist corruption may, ironically, be corrupted when they ascend to power, either by the tyranny of a populace demanding bread and circus or else a fear of vulnerability in face of the loss of political control. As a baron said in the common era, *absolute power corrupts absolutely.* Those who intend to defy corruption are corrupted, in turn, by the unsound means to their own ends, whether to safeguard their power in order to execute their ideals, even ones as benevolent as minimizing data overload, by resorting to harsh methods. In an axiom true to this day, sadly, this baron also noted, *history is not a web woven by innocent hands.*

Do you believe the junta existed?

Yes, I do.

Do you believe they're alive?

The water doctor pauses. As he lifts his short, square chin, choosing his words thoughtfully before speaking, his smooth head shines gently, a gateway of gray matter to an obscure realm of predigital arcana. He whispers under his breath. Alive or not, the vestiges of their non-regime, a regime existing all but in name, remains with those of us who survived the collapse. We cannot forget those whom the junta subjected to inhumane work hours in abysmal labor conditions prior to the genocide. Take, for instance, the mass divestitures. You've heard about the divestitures, haven't you? A noble cause, as the old moth-and-rust treasuries relied on outdated technology at the risk of pollution and diminishing fossil fuel reserves, despite the junta's excavation of a mass grave of mammoths under Uberasia. However, as I'm sure you know, the junta had no viable contingency plan for alternate energy sources—whether harnessing downslope foehn winds from global warming, boiling vats of high fructose syrup, or burning excess cellulite, those dimpled powerhouses of fat on no one's wish list.

What about using fruitbat guano as biofuel?

Don't you know? Bots are a major cause of dysthymia.

Not bots. I said bats.

Forgive me. My friend, I am not a pathologist. Regardless, I am wary of those nocturnal flying foxes of the air, those toothy fruitbats who poop all over this biome. Rabies, for one. The junta should've exterminated those legions who mass-invaded our urban jungle and looked to other renewable sources like hydropower or geothermal energy.

I see. Where are the junta today?

To this day, my wife will not walk under a candelabra tree, one of the favorite hiding places of the tree-hugging junta who were rumored to put their eyes on everything, everywhere, even in the hand-built tree houses of our childhood memories, with their wireless microsurveillance unyielding as limpets hugging a hydrothermal vent. You know what? The water doctor sniffs the air close to Yang's face. Excuse me. Please forgive me for saying so, but you smell very good. Friendly. Sort of like cakes my mother used to bake with a little bit of carob, and a drop of vanilla bean extract.

It's immunoglobulin.

Why?

It eradicates xenophobia.

You don't say.

An immunological prodigy gave it to me.

Do you wear it like a perfume?

Yes, precisely.

What do you seek from me?

Did the junta enhance the common good?

The water doctor shakes his head. Sighing, he frowns. For this interrogation, you might as well be one of them, he admonishes, wagging his long index finger in Yang's upturned face. A reformed one yourself, a gardener in our new economy of barter. You have no shame, no remorse about your reprobate history as a data-larded glutton, data-glutted sluggard, the brazen bourgeoisie of the digerati? Your own data-driven affluenza, driving the bots—the very souls and stewards of data—into underground exile?

Sir, I am a gardener.

Were you one of those quislings for the junta?

Sir, I didn't visit to pick a fight.

Let me ask you. Why was the underground resistance a hideout of spider-holes and spooky bat caves under the mezzopolis? Where is the maze of unseen catacombs for the brigades of zoomorphic bots? Why has no one mourned the abandoned brigades of chatbots, ferreting ferrets and data hounds, the firefoxes, jellyfish, and bee bots? As the cadres of bots lacked the minimal agency to mutiny, their number-crunching codes were doomed to self-destruction in an analog society. However, our denizens are more concerned about an existence devoid of bot chatter than the well-being of bots themselves.

And what do you believe, sir?

In a realistic figuration of the figuratively real.

A sign or a referent, sir?

No, not quite.

What do *you* think of the campaign, the great leap sideways?

What do I think, echoes the bespectacled water doctor, pursing his lips. Does what I think even matter in this destitute world of ominpresent, bloody vestiges of the junta's drumhead tribunals? Don't you see the mined fields of data casualties, sprawling from east to west, as far as the eye can see? That's where some of those mass executions occurred, night after night, until the muses were so bold, their Y-shaped slingshots ricocheted across the X-axis of broad daylight. Those datamined fields cry out with the blood of those who resisted brainwashing by sleep deprivation in the retronyming collectives. My counterintelligence work on the underground resistance triggered nightmares of a dystopic life as a scavenging bot scripted to smash discord to smithereens, and my subsequent bids to retool a civilization's lost memories out of fragmentary code. Believe me, bots don't have fun.

Why hasn't anyone recovered the bots?

The water doctor coughs. Are my thoughts original thinking, or are they preordained by the noospheric designs of the alpha and omega? In their turrets of thought-trafficking and catacombs of critical data, within mausoleums of decision-making misery, did the junta conduct any risk assessments or analyze direct evidence to inform their methods? Indeed, what about dead bots? Don't you know about the kangaroo courts in the mine-blasted, bloodfields on the outskirts of the mezzopolis? Are you one of those vigilantes, a lethal puppet of the junta? Did you engineer those water shortages and cloud outages? Did you meteorologically remaster our digitally programmed weather? Are you masquerading as a tenth muse, a pseudomuse of data? Did you, a tenth pseudo-muse—riding bareback astride a holographic stallion with stereoscopic infrared vision blazing at the rear of the junta while the muses galloped, veiled-and-wimpled with their flying habits, onto the information highways accompanied by those cryptography-secured blockchains dragged with an uproarious air of the carnivalesque in the wake of the junta's thundering hooves—did you, my friend, sell your one and only soul to this fulsome regime? What good did you believe would arise from destabiliz-ing the world's warehouses of data overnight? And what reboot plan did you outline in anticipation of the collapse of a crowdhosted, cloudbased commune enforced by the junta's harsh measures? Didn't you see the harm you'd cause? If so, how could you?

Please say no more, sir.

Silence.

Please tell me, sir.

Silence.

Tell me. What do you do nowadays, now that the water bowl is completed?

My friend, I can smell a red herring when you toss one into a logistics pool, but I'll graciously follow your digression. I'm handwriting a waterproof book for the post-digerati of my children's children's children, so my spawn can freely access a reservoir of wisdom surviving their great-great patriarch who lived through the digital expansion and its untimely collapse, and memorize the adage that information alone is neither good nor evil, but rather, the judicious hearts of those governing its systems must be fair and wise, the latter which I myself have yet to witness.

Sir, what do you know about the information wars?

Silence.

Do you believe the wars consisted of a series of battles in those years of biopolitical, fiscodigital, and epistemological catastrophes?

Silence.

Did the wars trigger the great regression?

Silence.

Why the hesitation, if I may ask?

Silence.

When was the last time you saw the minefields lying outside the mezzopolis?

Silence.

You have nothing to fear, sir.

Silence.

I am not one of the junta, sir.

Silence.

I am not a cloud.

Silence.

Please tell me. After the collapse, the viral paralysis meant that the junta, if extant, could no longer access the surveillance technology used to gather big, critical data to fuel predictive analytics, not to mention data-informed surveillance, for the minimization and the deregulations of our labyrinthine cloud system. Ironically, we needed data in order to reduce data overload. This meant that thousands, if not millions of denizens suffered withdrawal symptoms from their device addictions, if they didn't already overdose on fiscodigitalia before then.

Silence.

Sir, I came to inquire about your pursuit of happiness.

Silence.

I journeyed two days and two nights to find you.
Silence.
I slept on the shoulders of bombed-out byways.
Silence.
I drank umpteen bottles of microfiltered rainwater.
Silence.
I ate a peach grown by my own tree.
Silence.
Do you believe me, sir?
Silence.
Tell me about the information wars.

The water doctor inhales deeply, then closes his bespectacled eyes with a grave air, as if preparing to explain a complex theorem. In lowered tones, he says: The information wars weren't fought in a typical sense, not in the sense of cyberwars fought remotely or the bloody carrion wars of yore, and not even the spate of thousand-drone wars. The unholy ammunition consisted of exaggerated rhetoric and skewed lines of argumentation, *ad nauseum*, and the lives were lost to dogma without nuanced explorations of ideologies. In essence, the wisdom warriors were fierce polemicists. Over the data-logged concourses, we fought about intangibles magnified by battles over epistemologies in the dissolving multiversities. First, the scientific methods of observational study versus, secondly, our interpretation of human experiences, for instance, of jurisprudence, literature, history, art, music, ethics, philosophy, and philology with *literae humaniores*, and the vanishing studies of divinity notwithstanding. The information wars sought to answer questions about what types of knowledge were most meaningful, and whether meaning itself was, in fact, meaningful at all. In seeking these answers, however, a power struggle arose between our disparate modes of knowing, not to mention the silly ban on figurative language.

> Why silly, sir?
> Can we strip language of metaphors?
> Why would we?
> Is a cloud a cloud? A jellyfish a jellyfish?
> Do you believe the wars are still raging, sir?
> Yes, all over the world.
> What does this mean?
> Silence.
> Are we derived from nothing, designed for no purpose?
> No, my friend.
> How do you know, sir?
> *Caput inter nubilia.*
> Surrender to the clouds?
> One plunges one's head into the clouds.
> How so, sir?
> *Carpe noctum.*
> My Latin is rusty, sir.
> Seize the night, my friend.
> What about the day?
> Well, the saying is, *sol orietur.*
> Why seize the night, sir?
> Why are you so sure the sun will rise?
> I am a gardener.
> So am I, my friend, in a manner of speaking.

✦

After thanking the water doctor and bidding farewell with a handcrafted gift of pulverized baobab in exchange for jackfruit leather, then a conciliatory handshake, Yang embarks on his journey home, the cylinder of superfood baobab powder jouncing along in his burlap satchel. Slowly, he ponders his mixed feelings about the water doctor's darkling worldview by revising, in his mind's eye, a fragment of a poem he'd scribbled about apocalyptic weather and the collapse. He believes the little poems, not dissimilar to the logic puzzles of his boyhood, offer a safe zone of focus where he can set aside the nagging anxieties of the hour to meditate upon an imaginary object of symmetry and beauty. Architectures of imagination—one via imaginative empathy, the other via faculties of reason—assembled intricate patterns of words or numbers, and harmonized thinking with dreaming. Whether the junta enhanced the common good or not, Yang is grateful for the water doctor's insights, and forgives his new friend for the outbursts of inflammatory rhetoric.

✦

A MONOGRAPH OF
ESCHATOLOGICAL WEATHER

Dissertation on weather, a meterological almanac
        forecasts the millennium
           as I dash home without an umbrella—
quarto nylon-folds neatly sewn with salvaged
                ice-fishing lines, signatures
in a saddle-stitched bodice,
    a barometer of hand-blown glass on dust,
tidal moon—digital simulation of zebrafish
on zylonite,
            kettle-stitch of crystalline data
annealed to a hinge,
               deckle-edged sea wave,
        drum-leaf tender,
           X-rayed buckram, radiolucent
diamond on a radiograph film, glassine
    glue of wild-caught fish-bones
               or flyleaf isinglass.
Soon, the water doctor warns,
the second coming will deluge us with months of rain,
and this turn-of-century volume
          of apocalyptic phenomena—
dropped in a rain squall—
      shall be drowned in a bibliophile's
          dreamcloud of expansion
                  then deletion,
      the right to be forgotten.

Six | The Centenarian

THE CENTENARIAN

In this day and age, who would wish to be a hundred?
If a former denizen of data sees an angel
waiting in the future, then she might surmise

the angel with long, bell-shaped sleeves isn't real—
only speculation, but I daresay she sees
the angel as a sign of hope, a good design

in the alpha and omega of the universe
regardless of what life sets before one's eyes—
a platter of mirth and melancholy alike,

which the angel hides up her sleeve—
an elixir of life, the fountain of youth,
aqua vitae for those who drink bitters with sweet.

✦

The fourth harbinger of happiness, based on coordinates
deciphered from the black bento box, is a hundred year-
old person—a reclusive, left-handed koto musician who
dwells alone on a mesopheric tract of double-wide pods
near the leeward side of the mezzopolis. This woman,
a centenarian, apparently holds a secret to longevity. It

exists not in an elixir, a gene, an inhalable immunoglobulin, or even in the fine-grained wood of her silk-strung
zither, but rather, in a wellness cloudbit. Yang assumes it
is no longer functioning after the collapse. Indeed, the
junta's concerns about overpopulation and the shortage of energy sources were broadcast throughout the
fiefdoms, while whisper campaigns insinuated, on the
contrary, that abbreviated lifespans was a shadowy goal
of the junta's great leap sideways. Given the skyrocketing
mortality rates, Yang can't help wondering whether the
junta intended to reverse-engineer this woman's invention to shorten lifespans instead, but Yang does not mull
over the minutiae of conspiratorial lore. He prepares a
bamboo thermos of yerba buena infused with bergamot
and a gift of black sesame cakes, good for the gray matter
as well as long life, and for the tensile strength of silvering hair, of which Yang has a few premature strands.

✦

The more deeply Yang explores the shrouded world of the
junta, the less formidable yet more perplexing the nine
muses appear—how did the muses of postmodern herstory,
synthetic music, astrophysics or radioastronomy, romantic
comedy in stereo with love and comedy, epic poetry slam,
electrochoreography, post-traumatic memory, and domestic tragedy of the ages—with their utopic impulse to
boost happiness and maximize the common good with a
minimalist approach to data—indeed, how did these nine
muses grab power before nosediving so catastrophically,
fracturing the empire's oligarchy into fiefdoms, and finally,
hitting a nadir with the fiscodigital collapse? Did they re-
ally deliver those lethal, exploding candy grams? Did the

great leap sideways work, or did it inadvertently escalate workaholism and cause untimely deaths? Was it a case of muses-with-a-fury or so-called benevolent despotism? Did they deliver underground boxes of cellophane-sleeved flowers of regenerated cellulose—nasturtiums, larkspur, anemone, grandiflora roses, tulips the color of fire retardant—to console the bots or not? Did bots desire consolation? Was this a patronizing gesture or not? Or a pathetic fallacy? Did the junta actually revitalize the imagination and repel dysthymia? Did the junta successfully infuse the biosphere with lost virtues while vanquishing hedonism?

Speaking of which, what cruel message would blooming floribundas and grandifloras portray in a season of mass underground vanishings—nay, let's name it, dear reader—of genocide? Or did the nine muses themselves shapeshift into bots, a virtual feat of zoomorphism, then obliterate all traces of their own existence, and if so, why? Were the bots a figment of our collective *anima* or *animus*, the hazy archetypes of empiricism, female and male digerati of molecular amphoterism or hermaphroditic binarism? Why do questions about a bygone technocracy of fiefdoms matter when no one controls the biomasses clouding the biosphere anymore? (And while we mull over these mysteries, the maze of transparencies in the noosphere trembles ever so slightly with unmoored clouds like me, i.e. a hodgepodge of information without answers, or data set adrift without meaningfulness.)

✦

After listening to stories of denizens who wished to end their lives yet who, in a reversal of fate, survived their heart-dropping jumps from the skywalk, and where bok-choi is traded instead of proxy addresses or stocks and securities, Yang is especially keen on hearing the centenarian's story. In this collapsed age where fiefdoms have regressed to analog living, what post-traumatic memories of the junta's campaigns linger in the noggins of predigerati who lived prior to the rise of the empire? Why cultivate longevity in this cloudfree slough of despondency, anyway? His mother would've said, *chuán dào qiáotóu zì rán zhí.* The ship will reach the end of the bridge in due course. To paraphrase the angel of the future, what thought for tomorrow exists when today's darkness is roughly more or less enough?

Even in the heydey of the doomed fiscal bubble, the denizens in Yang's jellyfish network—exhausted from drowning in data—didn't show much interest in vitality but didn't wish to end their lives abruptly, either. In the zone of livestreamed monotony and automatic repetition, workaholism plugged a void in their souls while humble clouds such as I, hovering like minor angels in a maze of transparencies, understood that humanness meant risking a treacherous field of intangible emotions and disinformation. In other words, maybe due to their souls, humans seek more to life than sitting up late at night computing regional exarchate taxes, or holding vigil inside an information portal of flesh, blood, saline, and air called the body. Yet this portal of cosy warmth and muddiness is not a blessing in disguise: the delights of the moment can lead to drastic errors.

+

A small-framed woman of advanced years, true to her latitudinal and longitudinal coordinates, waits under the spreading shade of a persimmon tree, extending a slender hand as

Yang approaches. With a bow, Yang offers the gift of black sesame cakes.

Unde es?

My Latin is rusty, Yang apologizes.

¿De dónde eres?

No hablo, confesses Yang, regretfully.

Where are you from?

Yang gestures north, then west, oceanside.

Melba, as in peach pie.

I'm a gardener. Yang. By the sea.

Why?

Why garden? Or why the sea, ma'am?

Did you garden before the collapse?

More or less.

What do you grow?

Rutabaga, sorrel, broccolini....

Have you come to learn about wellness?

Yes. Why cultivate longevity?

Why not, Señor Yang? My cloudbit monitored not only blood pressure and glucose levels but an assortment of vitality indicators. After a giant slice of peach Melba drizzled with caramelized sugar and garnished with crème fraîche, or even during your sleep due to the dawn phenomenon of an overactive liver, the cloudbit would gather big, critical data to share real-time, predictive analytics to inform your decisions, minute by minute. It'd monitor your lipids, creatinine, thyroid, and your adrenaline, oxytocin, and cortisol levels, and even the photopupillary light reflex of your iris. For women in their fertility years, it monitored estrogen, FSH for follicles, lutropin for the corpus luteum, and progesterone.

Anything else, ma'am?

Your serotonin and dopamine levels for mood swings.

During your waking hours, it adjusted your hunger pangs by adjusting the levels of your gastrointestinal neuropeptides—reducing aliquots of hunger hormones—or nudging you with ringtones to take your ginkgo biloba, guzzle mineral water, and go to the gymnasium for *taiqi* and *qigong* with other denizens. If you showed high levels of adrenaline, it'd urge you to go to the float tanks instead of swallowing a fistful of opioids.

The welldome, you mean?

Yes. Not a gymnasium.

No worries.

A telltale sign of my age.

Did you cloudsource, ma'am?

Those of us who lived through the information wars had nothing to lose in the last days of the commonwealth. A collapse wasn't on our radar—how sadly naïve of us. The junta safeguarded the opensource biodata and envisioned a cloudfree lifestyle to which our new generations were not privy. The predigerati remember. The digerati don't, and whatever they do, wish to forget.

Didn't retronyming shrink our lexicon?

No, no. By distinguishing between analog and virtual words in the commonwealth, the retronyming increased our pool of denotative terms. This for that, that for this. Revised into this is this and that is that. Clearer than our fuzzy use of figurative language. By the word, cloud, did we mean a cloud-cloud or one of those other clouds? A raincloud or a cloudsource? And so forth. Retronyming clarified and disambiguated the ambiguities. The junta also resisted hyperregulation and launched minimalism. Minimization, I mean. The reforms, however, led to a web of entanglements which hastened the onset of the collapse. I once lived in a fiefdom, if you will, of minimization which devolved into a microcosmic bureaucracy of ineptitude. Garbage in, garbage out. Bad data wiped out a lot of our efficiencies.

I thought the minimization obliterated all that bureaucratic nonsense.

Our municipal infrastructure was fuzzy. What's the ancient adage? I forget the Latin. Dysfunction eats strategy for brunch, or something else. Here's an example of a bureaucracy of ineptitude. In my fiefdom, an onslaught of analytics would rain on us for no reason, while filtering networks would stagnate at noon because of the shortage of bots assigned to municipal logistics, making us vulnerable to massive attacks. Why didn't we more painstakingly monitor the brigades of those around-the-clock bots while minimizing data proliferation and viral epidemics? At peak usage hours, our sluggish networks sank in a quagmire of overload. In cryptopiggy banks, our mazuma was useless thanks to inflation while the doomed fiscal bubble ballooned like a jumbo cloudbuster at a big sales party.

Didn't the junta forbid longevity research, ma'am?

I don't believe anyone knew about my investigations.

The junta's eyes were rumored to be everywhere.

Biting into a black sesame seed cake, Melba smiles. This is delicious. Did you bake this yourself? Reminds me of my mother's cakes. When he was alive, my late spouse enjoyed baking, too. We baked friendship bread, which used starter dough we'd shared with others. I'll bet the junta knew exactly what we baked weekly. Or maybe I was so peripheral that my cloudbit flew under the radar, even if it flew in the face of the polity. Who knows? This bionic cloudbit boosted a person's wellness, as you say, so why not outlaw it? I should clarify that it did not actually prolong longevity, but rather, longevity is a side effect of vitality. Don't know whether the junta wished to shorten our lives. If they did, at least we could enjoy health in our brief years. I bet it made no impact on the empire's gross domestic byproduct of equally gross information overload.

Yang clicks his tongue sympathetically.

The cloudbit would remind you to shut your eyes. Breathe. Go to the float tanks in the welldome. Drift like a jellyfish, right-side up. Float like a sea tortoise, face-down. Put on your bluelight goggles and go back in visual memory to your childhood meadows. In this post-collapse world, where strangers show up to exchange red-leafed kale for a conversation or trade daikon tossed with shallots to shoot the breeze, I do not miss those summers of nausea in the mezzopolis when waves of spreadsheets backed out of the liquid data dumps and ruined my shag rug.

What's a shag rug?

Shag. Rug. Short-term aggregate funds for resource utilization groups.

Would you please show me, ma'am?

The collapse totally destroyed my rug. Shag, too.

Melba raises a veined left hand in a slant of light, her slate-gray eyes alight with star-fires named in the tongues of mythological nomenclatures now fading. Her phalanges move with dignified grace, remaining supple over a hundred years thanks to fish oil, deep breathing, and glucosamine. On the back of her hand, a cloudbit gleams like an insect's wing in the blanched light. You see this? She waves her hand brusquely as if interrupting a concertino, *allegro con brio*, a lively cadenza. It's silent, due to the collapse—it's only a chip of silicon jewelry now, a bit of outdated paraphernalia or *memento mori*. A souvenir of mourning.

Or a bionic raindrop without a cloud, says Yang.

It does store data in a cloud out there, but that's moot now. As a member of the predigerati, I was born and raised before the era of zebra-code tattoos. Tattooists were artists, not technicians. I rode my bicycle everywhere. I still do. I baked loaves of egg-bread with cage-free eggs, and sold the braided bread at the farmer's market in the city. We lived in suburbs once, didn't we. In my girlhood, I ate grilled mackerel—my favorite dish—with olive oil and sun-blushed tomatoes garnished with cilantro. No zebra scans at the market. Nowadays, I love to indulge in a square of 75% dark chocolate and a glass of oaky red wine at night. At least four times daily, I engage in a life-giving act to sustain happiness, such as swimming or martial arts, although I do miss going to the float tanks at the welldome. My time-tested genes are blessed with longevity. I inherited the four genes linked to longevity, including the one proven to extend the lives of fruit flies. I have type O blood, a lower risk of coronary disease. My aging heart is a biomedical engineer's dream of perpetual motion, she says, *the finite longing for the infinite*, as dead philosophers would say. In yesterday's world, our neurological brainware siphoned information out of the maze of transparencies and vice versa as we sallied forth, unblinking, into the biosphere. We are no longer tuned into the cyberverse, and the nine muses no longer hum their mesmerizing music in the biosphere.

So the key is diet, moderate exercise, and good genes?

Silence. A dragonfly glides overhead, circling.

Melba waves her hand, shoo. She puts the rest of a second black sesame cake, the size of an analog silver dollar, in her mouth and chews thoughtfully. This is good. I haven't enjoyed a good cake since my spouse was alive, when we used to sip caffeinated chlorophyll at the quaint Uberasian bakery on the boulevard. We drank enough chlorophyll, my love and I. We joked that our bodies, together, could harness the light. She continues, drones could shoot thousands of images, over a thousand days, but microsurveillance would never capture my soul: a girlhood where I rode my bicycle to koto lessons on the cul-de-sac, or gathered pebbles in a creek—before it was tainted with gasoline—quartz ranging from violet to sienna to butterscotch. Picked buckets of wild blackberries fat as toggle buttons, and strolled hand-in-hand with my first and only love through superblooming fields of goldenrod. Later, I taught lessons at the conservatory. My love studied astrophysics at the technology institute and researched the slowing of light—yes, light traveling at less than the speed of light. We ate fish out of the sea and grilled them, foil-wrapped, over glowing coals with our bare hands, right on the beach. When we married, we dined in bayside clam shacks before the shellfish were tainted with viruses. The beaches shimmered with real sand, not smart dust. The ocean belonged wholly to itself and the weather. When he died after forty-seven years of our marriage, twenty-three of those at the multiversity, I sent my loved one's ashes in a capsule to outer space—one of the junta's projectile burial campaigns—so he could fly among the stars.

Do you believe the junta existed?

I do. The nine muses aspired to reform unbridled chaos. Feckless and fabulous at the same time, yet never fickle, the muses resorted to outright force to defend their museological dogma of minimization. I suppose the her-story lesson is obvious. No one can force anyone to be happy. Secondly, reform must be shaped by grassroots wisdom as well as analytics, and not solely driven by bureaucratic efficiency or worse, ineptitude. Meaningful, lasting reform occurs from the bottom up, in the heartwaters of the denizens where communal memory flows like an underground river. And remember, *the heart has its reasons of which reason knows nothing*, as a philosopher and mathematician once said. I forget the Latin.

Pascal never said this in Latin, ma'am.

Please forgive me if I wax nostalgic. You know, this always puzzled me. Why didn't the muses ever appear to us? I was a musician, after all.

Silence.

Have you ever seen one of the muses?

Yang hesitates.

Did you go to their motorcades?

Yes, I did.

I did, too, but I never saw them. Did you? In a blur—a flash of veiled-and-wimpled fabric—the muses flew past us. Why did they cover their faces? Who is my muse? Why didn't the muse of synthetic music, epic poetry slam, or electrochoreography appear to me? I'm a classically trained, analog musician. Not even my spouse, an astrophysics professor at the multiversity, witnessed the muse of astrophysics at work in one of the million cubicles of mesophere.

Yang changes the subject. Why live to be a hundred?

If you harbor a gene for small cell carcinoma in the lungs, the cloudbit would trigger T cells to fight small cell carcinoma in the lungs. Why not try immunotherapy? If you wish to conceive a child in a graft of uterine epithelium grown *in vitro*, the cloudbit could help your body receive a petaled graft on your abdomen. Why not? Through a prognosis assessment, the cloudbit could trigger a stream of cells in a healing cascade to mitigate areas of vulnerability to environmental stress, such as a salvo of fruitbat guano right out of the sky. If your pancreas couldn't secrete enough insulin and glucagon, cells would migrate to the pancreas and differentiate swiftly into new islets. If you burned a hole in your retina by squinting at the sun's corona during an eclipse, cells would migrate to your fovea centralis. If you felt dysthymic, the cloudbit would moderate your serotonin uptake and instantly message you about the availability of float tanks at the welldome. If you did all these things and more, yes, perhaps you could live to be a hundred. Why not? Yet few denizens nowadays wish to live a century, due to the misery of cloudfree living.

Maybe the bees do.

Do the bees recall the collapse?

Maybe.

Does a bee know it's a bee?

+

A LITANY OF PRAISE
IF I LIVE A HUNDRED YEARS

Hear angels in a cloud upstairs, rustling
by the armchairs I rarely use, over a prayer
cushion I do not use often enough, I muse.
Love the lavender from my garden, wilted
from black rot in a spring deluge. I retain
brass child protective locks on the cabinets
though no one lives in my house, only bees.
Sea bright, the world blesses an aquarium
of sepia ink before the rain. A storm, hazing
a horizon line, spills a hem of summer indigo
aglimmer in the metallic thread of an evening
gown with a large, faux-diamond collar-clasp.
Who is brave enough to don the sea as garb?
My bones, especially in the shoulders, are too

small for it. I take humility in a dose of salt,
holy and granular. As swimmers disentangle
giant sea kelp longer than their own bodies,
we touch archipelagic gold among the morels,
new chanterelles in our garden of early fruit.
A cormorant winging rapidly over the waves
is not a sign, you observe. A bird is no more
than the meanings we assign to it as a word,
most meaningful to the hapless fish it eats,
who regards the last rink of the universe
from the recesses of the waterfowl's throat.
False modesty, garish flag of such a notion—
be wedded, soul and harbor, to the origins
of light and love itself, biogenesis of life.
Bless a grand, informational ocean, all in
charismatic splendor, a judicious room
of its own mossy reform. Offerings I carry
to the sea's shore on a rugged, gull-laced
rock-cliff—eucalyptus heartwood chopped
into wet fragments after a storm—dry it out,
says a carpenter, let the sun and salt cure it—
you can use it as firewood. Why undergo
this trouble for a little flame, a bit of wood,
I wonder. At a hundred years of age, I eat
all the skin on the fish without worrying
about fats, good or bad, adrift
                    in my centenarian blood.

Seven | The Listening Artist

THE LISTENING ARTIST

The art of listening is a nautilus, a gouache cut
out of your inner ear, a snail in negative space, a spiral

of hunger coiled like a fiddlehead in one soul
     gazing at another to say—

whatever you pick up as music or earworms
without our hands or drums, in the absence of stars,

navigating this cloudbased life
     in the manner of an atlas moth

whose cocoon is spun for silk, who soars
     on those imaginal discs it yielded

as a juvenile to grow an abdomen,
     an adulting thorax, and zany antennae—

dazzles even the most empirical of digerati.

✦

Momentarily distracted by the howling sea wind outside his shanty, rattling the roof salvaged from an analog

junkyard, Yang is worried that the fifth harbinger of happiness may not actually exist due to a referential ambiguity. This lack is not due to a flaw in the junta's algorithms or Yang's methodical calculations, but rather, a concern regarding a geographical location that no longer, apparently, exists. Thanks to global warming and greenhouse gases, the overheated networks short-circuited in this section of the mezzopolis a while ago, and the empire did not allocate sufficient mazuma to repair the damaged infrastructure. With the gravity and decorum of a postdigital pilgrim, Yang decides to make the trek to the nine hundredth district where cybernightlife once buzzed under the omnipresent eyes of the junta, even in those innocuous light-emitting diodes strung on miles of optic fibers across the sky, transmitting big data by the nanosecond.

✦

The mezzopolis of ghosts without footprints, a pixel-free exposition bereft of throngs of looky loo tourists, reminds Yang of an abandoned pseudocarnival devoid of fantastical blimps and exotic creatures on a brackish riverbank of turn-of-century effluvia, spooked by spectral warehouses refurbished into boutiques with zippered sleeping-pods and aerial bed-and-breakfasts overlooking the biomass. The junta's welldome, which subsidized cloud-gardens and float tanks with seed monies, ultimately failed due to a dearth of both supply and demand, i.e. no gardeners, no mazuma, no clouds in the season nearing zeroization. The denizens wanted data for their dysthymia, not bread and circus. (Or in parallel translations, bread and pageants, bread and carnivals, bread and bazaars.) In the fiefdoms, no one applied for seed-funds to sow into their rutabaga plots, rosemary hedges, or genetically modified broccolini gardens. Rather, the analog seeds and crudité roots were exchanged by hand, not cloudfunds, *per se:* analog blackberries, cauliflower, real strawberry vines, zucchini seeds, fennel, sorrel, and fingerlings.

Forget me, forget-me-not. During the minimization, the junta's designs to reduce data overload by promoting the right to be forgotten, or more accurately, the right to forget all your superfluous data, failed miserably, a tragic tale often told with doses of disinformation wherein the words labyrinthine, draconian, and byzantine were quoted frequently. To this day, the lightrail no longer runs all the way to the end of its destinations. (In fact, it no longer runs.) The sky vacuums of the great leap sideways, frozen in mid-air, no longer whisk away petabytes of data to the clouds. For those with inborn optimism, however, any crisis is another dawn, cleverly disguised—*haec olim meminisse iuvabit*, or one day, this will please us to remember. At the very minimum, Yang reminds himself, this, too, shall pass. However, what can we truly predict about tomorrow, with or without data, and the subsequent tomorrows after that? Another supper of microdiet greens topped with shaved radish, another noon of weeding the rutabaga plot for bartering at the ragbag the week after next—everything is relatively superlative: most nourishing of shea butter soap for the most hexagonal of wax honeycombs, the spiciest of chilis for the ruddiest of pomegranates, the mellowest of melons for the crispest heads of butter lettuce, the mildest of yellow bell peppers for the cheekiest of pumpkins, et cetera.

✦

Although Yang is vaguely skeptical about listening as an art form like digital choreography rather than a social behavior or soft skill, he is willing to set aside his own biases. In particular, Yang doubts the survival of so-called listeners in a quarter gentrified by the digerati, later populated by ill-reputed bordellos where cybernightlife sizzled, depending on whom you ask and in which fractioned area of the mezzopolis. With a wrapped gift of dorayaki in his satchel—little buckwheat pancakes the size of sand dollars and filled with azuki, red-bean paste—Yang follows the tramway to the very end of the ward, putting one weary flipflop in front of the other, then crosses a river gorge on a suspension bridge, a braided swing of jute ropes. In this portion of the biome, the microclimate is subtropical, the air rife with hummingbirds. Robust, broad-leafed banana trees and plaintain groves flourish on both sides of the gorge, and fresh water trickles from exposed roots, plunging onto flatrocks fringed by giant ferns.

✦

A lost art, grumbles the listening artist who sleeps on a cot among hobnailed milk-glass dishes in a kitchenette pod on the other side of the lightrail. Who listens? I've oodles of idle timespace. No inheritance to manage, no bags of opioids grabbed by the junta, no dyspepsia and no one to mourn. Dysthymia, I mean. Before the rise and fall of the junta, I had a bit of mazuma stashed in my cloudfund for the underoccupied, a euphemism for the unemployed. You see, I missed the benchmark on the vocational assessment—scoring neither in cyber-collar nor blue-collar ranges, I was assigned to breathe for a living. I thought, if I scored any lower, would I not have to breathe? I don't enjoy those false dichotomies, and I don't believe in quotas or quotients—live and let live is my philosophy. Not long ago, in the days of my youth, before the rise of data tyranny, I played a B flat cornet, designed to make love to your inner ear, outlawed by the muse of synthetic music who denounced it as offensive, alongside the saxophone. In turn, I decried the muse's lyric mimesis as retroactively synthetic— aesthetically retrograde—not authentically cybersynthetic, deplorably so.

So you believe the junta existed?

Yes, I had a tiff with the muse of synthetic music, who communicated with me through a lamellophone mouth-harp. Wraith-like with silver-blue hair like silicon circuitry, she'd get upset when I played all sorts of gigs as a stranger adrift in a world of hungry hearts. After we parted ways, she'd text me indigo valentines with bleeding roses, arrows—indigo for indignant. A byte of a crazy poet in her, too.

Are you sure she was one of the muses?

No, I wasn't ever sure any female wasn't. When I emigrated from the other hemisphere to the west, I discovered that women thought my forehead—flat as a butter dish because my stepmother wouldn't pick me up when I was a baby—gave me a distinguished, patriarchal air and assumed I was a male of affordable means. So I was misjudged by antiquated phrenology, i.e. fake science of the predigerati. I bombed the suite of vocational assessments by refusing to compute the area of an octagon. I also failed to calculate compounded interest for the equations in the financial category. I'm too cynical to serve as a happiness planner alongside pink-clouded bots. Didn't know what a baker's dozen was, and don't care, so I couldn't be microcredentialed by the culinary institute of technology to work as a cyberbarista. Wasn't sorry that I missed the benchmarks for those, either. The muse of domestic tragedy abolished all jobs with a starting salary of less than this-and-such mazuma, and the muse of epic poetry slam was a prima donna who hogged the open mikes so no one else had a chance to flow. For the junta, I delivered heart-shaped candy grams—death threats for those accused of data overmining. You know, the nine muses were notorious for squashing dissension and sowing seeds of disinformation.

Why do you listen?

The art of listening is my groove. When I first moved to the mezzopolis, I was idle. With nothing much to do aside from my gigs as a jazz artist, I knocked on portals to deliver exploding valentine candy grams—subpoenas actually tantamount to death sentences—for the junta. Muses, I mean. Poof, each denizen vanished in a wink of a wiki as a candy gram burst into a cloud of dyed sugar. On my rounds, I became known as a neighborly soul who was invited to sit indoors and listen to the stories of jumping off the skywalk, of dazzling scions of the digerati and the daughters of affluenza, the dyspeptic and dysthymic, and those whose cells were furtively gleaned at birth to generate tissue for the organ trade. Although I was tantamount to the death angel in a metonymic sense, no one feared me. From jazz, I'd learned to soothe via easy listening. I spoke to them in a dead tongue which I studied as a schoolboy under the commonwealth, thanks to my immigrant father who was a classics scholar of the ancients before the common era. I would say, *qua patet orbis:* as far as the world extends. I would whisper, *non nobis solum,* not for ourselves alone. I would utter, *lucem sequimur,* we follow the light. My listeners failed to recognize this extinct language and its *memento mori,* artifacts as omens of demise, aphorisms of memorials and monuments, of undersea grottoes and the junta's mottoes. As you know, later on, this tongue was adopted as the spy language. My favorite axiom is, *quidquid Latine dictum sit altum videtur,* hah hah. Whatever is uttered in Latin sounds deep, hah hah.

You served candy grams on behalf of the junta?

Yes, I did.

Do you believe in the minimization dogma of the junta?

Who cares?

Do you believe in the right to be forgotten?

My data points no longer exist, yet I do.

Do you consider yourself a mercenary?

I listened to a man who was a fisher of data when the information sea not yet an unsustainable vat of unfiltered knowledge. He sat in a lighthouse on an archipelago, where it was rumored he could see bioluminescent angels—perhaps the algal tide, perhaps not—guiding squid boats to shore at night. He lost his son, his wife, and his mother in the information wars, and only his father lived, a tortured survivor of the retronym labor collectives whose nightmares of the milk-blossoming eyes of the dead—bliss of green-bottle flies who devoured carrion, not data— haunted him in daylight, years after solitary confinement. The sun would flash emerald as it dropped into the sea, yet the rare green flash was a good omen he no longer trusted after the ideals of the junta proved to be fallow in light of their unsound methods.

Is this a yes or no?

I listened to a bioengineer who transplanted hydrogel corneas onto eyes. The hydrogels, designed in the heyday of the commonwealth, displaced the demand for donated human corncas harvested from cadavers. We could no longer fabricate artificial corneas under the junta's cloudfree reform. The bioengineer performed the transplants illegally on the organ market with the assistance of bioinspired microrobots, whose zoomorphism into swimming hydrozoa and flying hymenoptera would render them invisible—or at minimum, elude surveillance monitoring by the junta. A girl with a corneal laceration would see again without searing pain or chronic scarring as she blinked. A woman afflicted by a degenerative corneal disease received her sight in full. A boy with an inflammatory eye condition would open his eyes to a windowless room's rose-colored light, the ruby color of blood leakage vanishing like a laser.

Do you believe in the zoomorphism of the bots?

I do. The bots, our souls of information, could also transmogrify into any zoological shape, figuratively speaking. Aquatic polyps, hydras, jellyfish medusas, wasps, drones, ferrets, hounds, and bees due to their ingenius facility with quantitative reasoning and data manipulation—from the gelid fractals of marine hydrozoa and turquoise-frilled, latticed sinophonophores to golden catacombs of honey-secreting workers, why not? And why not humanoids, in the phyla of all things? If we once lived inside clouds, why were the bots forced to work in darkness? And what did we gain as a result of their loss?

What else have you learned?

Despite a strictly timed regimen of hormones

injected through hollow needles the size of horse syringes, deep breathing, and twilights spent in float tanks, a middle-aged woman couldn't conceive. While in favor of revitalizing aging eggs in the egg banks, the junta had banned in vitro fertilization while endorsing uniparental oocyte fusion in an exploration of humanoid parthenogenesis. At last, shortly after she and her spouse gave up, she conceived a child the old-fashioned way. On the sonogram, a baby lima bean. In size, I mean. After the third month, however, the fertility specialist reported no heartbeat. By that time, the child was a soybean pod, the size of big ones from the archipelagoes of Uberasia. The woman wept for days afterwards, inconsolable, after which her spouse, frustrated by her acute dysthymia, attempted to jump off the skywalk, but was hauled to safety by the angel of the future. The woman bought a cypress hinoki soaking tub, poured hot darjeeling by the kettleful in it, and sat in the tub for hours, thinking she should procure a miniature therapy pig like the ones servicing memory-loss facilities for the elderly. Pigs are lifelong learners who harbor episodic memories, and their little grunts are soothing. When she arose from the tub, her body was the color of henna and deoxygenated blood, an auburn rosette whose horse-syringe pricks to the belly amounted to a trail of grief.

Silence.

The listening artist bites slowly into a dorayaki, tasting the azuki paste. Buckwheat pancakes instead of the typical sponge cake sweetened with mizuame, liquid barley malt? This works, I think. Never thought of using buckwheat instead of mizuame syrup, which my mother used. You're creative. You know, I listened to an analyst, not one of the gardeners who scaffolded the mezzopolis with their virtual infrastructures, but a vintage analyst with roots in the talking cure, dialectical behavior therapy—she clarified, wherein you talk to yourself, not just somebody else—the cure developed at the turn-of-the-century before the invention of mood-monitoring cloudbits, before the rise of psychopomp and neurodivergence, to boot. The analyst's only son died in the information wars, during battles over literally who-knows-what in those years of bio-political, fiscal, and epistemological turf. And everything in her pod was a mess, as her spouse left her for a cyber-strategist in an exarchate of Uberasia, and she relied on genetically modified algal caffeine. Despite the loss of her son in an overseas data dump, the analyst believed neither data overload nor its minimization would be our demise.

Did the junta offer any reparations?

No. I listened to those who survived the junta's retronym labor system, in essence a penal colony where denizens lived on a macrodiet of microgreens while tasked with a tedium of miniscule chores. I mean trivial, mind-numbing tasks like deleting all nouns germane to retire-ment and pension from lexicons to counting the grassroots clouds hosted in gardens—those cultivated by yesteryear's digerati—plus those clouds owned and operated by mo-nopolies. And the denizens confined in the junta's retro-nym collectives not only edited the lexicons, but rounded up dead bodies—deceased from karoshi, exhaustion from overwork—in underground necropolises to the nearest tenth of a decimal, rewarded only by more shovelfuls of meaningless yottabytes and zettabytes.

And those who believe the retronymed lexicons en-hanced our language?

I listened to gardeners, your ilk and kind, as you say. I listened to the hypnotic buzz of hidden bots whose bellies were slaked with dirty data. Yes, in listening to gardeners speak of their banished others, the bots, I sensed rage mixed with relief at their own preservation in the fiefdoms as vigilantes and retronymists, and their guilt at the degradation of their doppelgängers, the foraging bots excommunicated from cloud-gardens. If the junta believed that the lungs of the earth were wholly cloudbased, why did the muses abuse those who mined data on a daily basis? Who would clean up the bad data and stop the cycle of garbage in, garbage out? Minimization. In my mind's eye, the glowing abdomens of worker bees, ones who ceaselessly gathered cross-tabulated data flowering out of a fractured empire, rose on the wings of drones over luminous rivers of toxic honey. Bees, yes, lovely bees of transparency and virtue, humming and swirling in a sea of information.

What about the flowering of metaphorical language, banned in the wars?

We can't avoid using metaphors. We can't deflower language. That's ridiculous. There is no improvisation to my listening, no riffs, no singing, but language is innately figurative. Something stands for something else: we can't get rid of that metaphorical impulse. It's poetry. I listened to a girl, an immunological prodigy, who was disturbed by the abuse and exploitation of bots as recounted by her mother—shapeshifting bots overworked in web colonies, excommunicated by the junta. Exiled, I mean, toiling in utter darkness. This girl was a poet, I tell you, wise beyond her years. And the bots were classified in a figurative manner, analagous to the animal kingdom: bees, ferrets, hounds, firefoxes, jellyfish, the list goes on. I do not believe the junta ever delivered boxes of tulips and roses with beautiful names—the hybrid varieties, I mean—with human names like Julia and Aiko and Lily and Xing. The consolation of flowers was a myth. No one warned the bots about the junta's ultimate plan to purge every bit and byte of their buzzing genius in the minimization.

Do you think the bots were data subjects?

Ideally, yes.

What do you do with the stories you hear?

Nothing.

What about those indigo valentines?

Nothing.

Can I believe anything you've told me?

No.

Are you aware that you've exhibited conversational narcissism, please forgive me—by ignoring the majority of my questions?

No, I'm not.

Is shooting the breeze an art, if you don't listen?

Silence.

You delivered candy grams.

Yes, I did.

You listened to each victim's story, knowing each one was a target.

Yes.

Each victim knew your face.

Maybe.

Do you consider yourself a mercenary?

No, I don't.

Did you sell or trade their woes to the googolplex gazette?

Maybe I'm a bit of a narcissist, but I'm not a mercenary.

Why not?

Did I make mazuma at the expense of anyone's ethics?

Are you proud of what you were paid to do?

I served only as a messenger.

You knew them each by name.
They're not victims. Each candy gram was a valentine.
A valentine, sir?
A muse's love note delivered by a listening artist.
Love has nothing to do with this.
Love is as strong as death.
Silence.
Why should I prove anything to you?

LOVE MONOLOGUE TO AN UNSOLVED PROOF

Listen, after a digital apocalypse,
please find me. I shall dig us out
without a waterproof proof, ergo

where a rainy axiology blooms,
where our silver-haired sages wax
dialogical in a field of nonlinear

musing. In an age of logical fallacy,
we never know anything for certain.
Who wonders what fate will befall

validity, vulnerable in a firestorm?
Our abstracts shot to zero, thought
experiments of cats dead yet alive,

arguments rolling at sea, a riptide
where low cries of nihilists vanish
in a final proof by fire or flood.

In any case, maybe by listening,
I promised you love. At least,
a monologue germane to love,

which means, in this stanza,
mere repetition of *love* and *love*
while you read, dear reader.

Eight | On War and Peace, Redux

ON WAR AND PEACE, REDUX

You cannot see the war from this seaside garden—
     yet one draws nigh: a swelling tide
         of algal biofuel and God.
By night, the mantle of a ruined world glows
           in its flaming, cavernous heart.
By noon, a glow-torch bougainvillea
       dies in the arms of fall, then regenerates
in the spring. An analyst, whose son did not return from the
war, plants
         a single non-fruiting olive,
     virginal in its fire resistance, serene in its immunity
to xenophobia and famine alike. Is it not a waste to fight what
attacks over
      and over, a terminal disease, a relentless vector of hate?
The analyst says, this war, too, is my ravaged son: One moment
in history
        is the desolation of centuries
             of unwitnessed violence.
     The one who goes to war,
        and one who instigates war,
    in the end, are one
    and the same: the same one who dies, one way
       or another. *Aliquid stat pro aliquo*—
    something stands
        for something else.

✦

Either in a serendipitous turn of fate—cherries aligning in a randomized bonanza of happenstance, or thanks to an algorithm underlying the junta's clouds of prophecy, the analyst mentioned by the listening artist surfaces in the ensuing set of geographic coordinates.

In his satchel, Yang puts a bamboo thermos of gyokuro tea—to boost theanine with anxiety-blocking properties, shaded bushes are covered with reed screens before harvesting—and chia seed pudding flavored with almond milk, all served in a coconut shell. An analyst, thinks Yang, would certainly provide straightforward answers concerning questions of happiness after the collapse.

✦

The analyst is not a scientist, not a data analyst of yore but rather, a psychotherapist who owns a foxing, moldering facsimile collection of turn-of-century case studies by the cocaine-sniffing patriarch of the talking cure. First trained in the venerable art of dialogue, this analyst was recertified via distance licensure in R-BOT or reboot overload therapy, a type of cognitive behavior therapy proven effective for managing distress triggered by data overload, a nervous condition which merited its own category in the updated, unexpurgated Data and Statistical Manual of Macroviral Disorders or DSM-MD, which omitted the multiaxial subcategories of diagnosis. By way of fiscodigital explanation, the muse of post-traumatic memory was mercilessly goaded by the moguls of megacorporations to mask the overdiagnosis of dysthymia, in turn disguising the damaging effects of data dumping in the sea of disinformation. Says the analyst, dryly, her bird's nest hair in bobby pins, I drink my chlorophyll black nowadays, strong and dark as a new spring moon, wherein photosynthesis is a genetically modified dream of wakefulness.

✦

With a bow, Yang offers the chia seed pudding.

I lost my only son in the wars, sighs the analyst, as if telling the story for the umpteenth time in a discombobulated pod where chlorophyll mottles the polyacrylic storage cubbies and buffed pseudoquartz sinkboard. The analyst puts a spoonful of the chia seed pudding in her mouth. Isn't this marvelous? I haven't tasted chia seed pudding in a while. Did you flavor it with hemp, soy, coconut, or cashew milk? I live on caffeinated chlorophyll. The algae harnesses light and hydrogen dioxide and makes caffeine as well as iron, copper, and vitamin B.

Actually, I take my caffeine in green tea.

Gazing at Yang with warm gravity as she speaks, the analyst swallows and continues. In the battles over the slippery usage of figurative language, the automated drones of Uberasia, our fiefdom on my father's mother's side, killed my son in so-called friendly fire. *What sort of friendly fire is this?* I thought when I received the message. To this day, I despise euphemisms and non-denotative uses of words for this very reason, yet I cannot shed my instinct for analogy and metaphor-making. Buried in an unmarked data dump overseas, my son is forgotten by a cloud of witnesses. The eighth muse did nothing except to drop little vials of sky-blue trapezoids, namely, serotonin reuptake inhibitors, at the portal of my sleeping-pod. Due to global warming, the mass deaths of evergreens caused a ban on wreaths, so my son and other men and women who fought in the campaigns of the wars could not receive a wreath-laying ceremony. To honor his life, I transplanted this virginal, non-fruiting olive tree from a greenhouse in this biome.

What about a flag ceremony or a salute?

What flags? Rituals no longer mean anything in this new order, and we don't use analog flags anymore. Don't you know? With the shortage of textiles, the oligarchy confiscated flags for use as clothing in the outlying exarchates where the wars raged. It's where the junta's pirated stash of sensory boutique rubies served as a bunker, the locale where they leveraged their power, even with connectivity available only in the wee hours. Yes, galloping in their veils and starched wimples a squadron ahead of the flower-wielding masses on the boulevards, applauded by our idealogues and biorevolutionaries, the junta triggered this present crisis of meaning. Our capacity to extract import and beauty from monotony, or elicit value and significance out of sequential ordeals, eroded as their control only compounded the neurasthenia and paralysis triggered, ironically, by a surfeit of analytics. In other words, what minimal iota of data will identify which superfoods will reduce my dysthymia? What shall I wear to impress the digerati? Are these supplements made of pulverized freshwater pearls or fabricated pearlescent glass? Based on my sequenced genome, who am I, and what shall I do?

Ma'am, I'm very sorry about your son.

Goes without saying. Spirulina?

I'm a tea-drinker.

Of course. You see, my son loved tea. Lemon verbena tea steeped with chamomile flowers before he went to sleep as a boy, as he was afflicted by the free-floating anxieties of his generation, and favored the homeopath remedies of floral aromatherapy and reading aloud by candlelight to usher him into an analog dreamcloud. He disdained the hydrogel lenses mandated by the commonwealth that would monitor fluctuations in his mood. *I don't know why I feel the way I do, but I know what I feel,* he used to say. He loved the honeysuckle vines blossoming at dusk, frothing with heady perfume—or was it the star jasmine that was nocturnal? To be honest, my memory of his boyhood blurs, so it's good to say these things aloud. He loved radioastronomy. I bought him a sky telescope when he was seven, when his goal was to discover and name a comet. At the age of nine, he could explain how a googol was ten raised to the one hundredth power, so log base ten was one hundred. As the information wars in the outlying exarchates raged on, my son had inklings that one day, he might go. He would say, without understanding his words, *one day, I would like to be a martyr.* My son collected words like exotic flavors—*martyr* was one he learned by himself, which I saw him outlining with a stylus on liquid crystal. *Borborygmus* for the gurgling of intestines, and *digerati* for the datasophists in general. *Soteriology* for the doctrine of salvation after the common era. In retelling my loss, I find little comfort, but I'm grateful to have seen him flourish while on earth.

Aren't you an analyst?

Not that kind of analyst.

What do you mean, ma'am?

Not a data analyst.

No, an analyst of analysands.

Yes. Once upon a cloud, I used dialogue and scripting to coax my analysands out of their neurotic closets and agoraphobic boxes, yet I feel useless in talking aloud, myself. With the shift towards neurophysiology and psychiatric medicine, the talking cure was marginalized, besides. Even my own son floundered with face-to-face dialogue, straining to focus on a ping-pong game of back-and-forth verbalizations. Sorry, I cannot forgive his paternally useless spawner of narcissism, my estranged spouse, who deserted me after our son's passing to wander this earthly clod of mud embellished with data dumps. In the last days of the commonwealth, we harbored an innocent hope that the junta would liberate us from tyranny. In the end, what did we gain? War rather than peace, redux? A panegyric of positivism? Bravery? The right to be forgotten? And in the the glitzy piazzas of Uberasia, translated into our Anglophone tongue, *here lies an unknown soldier known only to God.* You know, in the last days of the commonwealth, I journeyed to one of the piazzas to see whether an inner witness would murmur within, this is your son. When I arrived, I stared at the marbleized sarcophagus while noctilucent rainclouds ushered in a falling dusk. As icy rain started to wet my face, panic arose: *They've taken my son, and I do not know where he lies.* I had no umbrella or rain kerchief. I walked alone in the rain of the piazza of the pod-hotel, weeping while the rain streamed on my cheeks, mixing hot tears with chilly rivulets. Tell me, what did we gain, my friend? This world of unplugged circuitry, rusting infrastructure, and lost clouds?

The end isn't here yet, ma'am.

Silence.

The olive tree in your yard will never bear fruit, yet it is beautiful.

Silence.

It won't live forever, but it might outlive you.

Silence.

Our lives are more than the deaths we carry daily.

Silence.

I'm very sorry about your loss, ma'am.
Silence.

✦

Of all the visits to the junta's harbingers of happiness, Yang
is most disconcerted by this woman's tale of woe. Deeply
moved yet startled by the intensity of the analyst's despair,
Yang feels perplexed at what the nine muses intended to di-
vulge through the analyst's tale of irrevocable loss, obviously
not overlooked by the muses of post-traumatic memory and
domestic tragedy due to her inclusion in the black bento
box's suite of algorithms.

Yang lifts his face to a blind sky where a colorless wind
imparts the odor of a coffin soaked in biofuel, decaying
roses, an overhead colony of musty, flying bats, and greenhouse gases. Beyond our middling sun—an average-sized
sun among zillions of suns, nothing special—the silent dark
flora of the universe, a velvet field edging a creek of stars
glowing in lily-bright gullets of milk, reveal nothing. (Yet
the noosphere flickers, apparently, with an average of a hundred billion neurons per human brain, as numerous as the
stars in the Milky Way.)

✦

As Yang walks away from the analyst's pod towards the outskirts
of a mezzopolis shrouded in depixelated haze like a ghostly,
skeletal ship kissed by ball lightning, he wonders—did he make
a mistake? Did he miscalculate and therefore incorrectly
decode the algorithms in the junta's black bento box? Was
the analyst supposed to be somebody else? Was the data
outdated, captured before the son's death, when her child

was alive and the analyst was happy? Was she ever happy? In Yang's mental flowchart of logical, reasoned tasks, he second-guesses himself. The questions lift off, one by one, like weather balloons into a cloud of spinning electrons and mounting storms detected by the barometer of his overactive sinus—which reacts with sneezing—yet unseen by the naked eye, like intangible corpuscles of happiness.

Yang muses silently. Am I reduced to a rigged sampan of forty-four bones, one for each year of life floating in time? Bone on bone, I've lost one hundred sixty-two of my two hundred six adult bones, reduced from two hundred seventy when I was a boy, before a smattering of bones fused while my body matured. How does the abode of our roiling emotions become equated with the trauma itself, the aggregation of wingless deaths until we succumb to a dimming of diodes on this polymorphic stage of a disquiet biomass, equipped to procreate within genetically engineered pools, but not to engineer anything *de novo* to save ourselves, this pseudonymized brouhaha of endlessly looping dysthymia?

✦

Yang does not wish to judge the analyst but feels negatively unsettled that a dialectical behavior analyst should appear so depressed after the collapse. Her sorrow flowed viscously as a lyotropic crystal in liquid form, the clouded hues of detergent mingled with seawater. As if Yang spies a montage of their life exchanges through the wrong end of a telescope, flickering in an old-fashioned cathode ray, melancholy is a grieving mother lying on a bed of hearse-black lilacs under a milky river of stars of unrehearsed rage, the hottest furnaces in existence yet farthest of lights. For the time being, fervent valentines in the universe murmur the name of one who cannot be recalled from an underworld of the dead, where the darkest lilacs will never unfurl their petabytes. (A lilac is an acronym for leading improvements in living austerely without cryptography.)

In other words, if the analysts are dysthymic, what are other denizens to do? What about the junta galloping up and down the concourses, veiled-and-wimpled—where did they go, and how did their livelihood change? Why did no one except the listening artist see their faces? What about the other angels of data, i.e. the ones of invention, of translation? As for the analyst's young son, one of millions drafted into the information wars, one of millions whose lives were robbed, killed, and destroyed by the commonwealth, wars which the junta later denounced as mass murders, i.e. crimes of the empire, Yang believes it's extraordinary, if not outright perverse, to classify this fallen warrior's plight as one of the keys to happiness. A mystery, perchance more so than the junta's inclusion of a death angel—one of many alleged death angels—the listening artist, encrypted within the algorithms of a lacquered black bento box.

✦

Looking over his shoulder, Yang takes one last glance at the non-fruiting cultivar in the analyst's yard, an olive tree which will grow sapwood and sage-colored leaves brightening in the sun yet which will also bear no fruit in the next hundred years, and none in the next, if it survives. Nonviolent in its poise, unaware of war or peace and the abatement of evil or the pursuit of virtue—this virginal olive tree, in post-digital solitude, yields a glimpse of redemption that Yang could neither fully articulate nor clearly define, except an elusive premonition that we might all return to see one another

again, not in this season but rather, a time known only to
the alpha and omega.

$+$

ALIQUID STAT PRO ALIQUO

The one who goes to war,
        and one who instigates war,
   in the end, are one
   and the same: the same one who dies, one way
       or another. *Aliquid stat pro aliquo*—
   something stands
         for something else.

Nine | The Happiness Machine

THE HAPPINESS MACHINE

No happiness machine exists,
yet we hear of this-and-such

a man trying to invent one—

A converted dreamcloud,
a light on inside

even when the door closes.
Letters of blessing and good will

in glass bottles overseas.

A retired heart-lung machine
circulates air not blood

in a sleeping-pod. Is this

happiness—to live in one's
own skin, breathing? Why

do we wish

to take this good
for granted?

✦

THE MAZE OF TRANSPARENCIES

An agoraphobic archivist who emigrated from a mossy southern biomass where part of his ancestral haplogroup died out in the information wars, who survived by swimming across the sea of disinformation, has allegedly designed a happiness machine. No such thing exists, thinks Yang, but he willingly suspends disbelief to satisfy his curiosity. A happiness machine. It purportedly dispenses aliquots of the elusive nonchemical substance, i.e. corpuscles of happiness. Not capsules, not ink leaflets or digital badges, and not as a vapor: rather, out of a wireless docking station for dreamclouds, an anchored replicator port the size of a cigar box inadvertently banned during the wellness campaign along with smokeless merchandise like nicotine vapor, mood-modifying inhalants, and epoxy resins mimicking estrogen, i.e. bisphenol A. Now it sits innocuously as a piggy bank in a corner of the pod of a wolfish man who originated it. (Mastermind is his title of choice, not inventor, designer, or innovator. According to the microbiography, his agoraphobia is a direct result of his displacement, and managed through alternative dreamcloud therapy.)

According to his customary practice, Yang packs a bamboo thermos of sencha infused with rose-hips and wraps a gift of glutinous sticky rice dumplings in a banana leaf. Pleased with how the dumplings turned out, neither too sticky nor too soft, Yang wonders whether the inventor of a happiness machine might turn out to be a curmudgeon who might not enjoy dumplings. If the analysts are dysthymic, what's an archivist to do? And what is a happiness machine, anyway? Although skeptical, Yang's curiosity propels him onto the next stage of his journey.

+

The mastermind of the happiness machine, once employed at the multiversity, dwells in a round pea-shaped pod tucked inside the rotunda of a smog-eating cybrary where he served as the head of obfuscation. (The crazed wrens and sparrows of the mezzopolis, who've sensed little change in the biome except for a trivial shrinking of electromagnetic fields, nest with aplomb. The armies of fruitbats, occupying a different nook in the rotunda, leave them alone.) After the reform campaigns by the junta in the midst of minimization, the archivist doggedly persisted in digging for the obscure essentials of happiness by analyzing big, critical data in dreamclouds the shape of oblong helium balloons. Maybe he could reverse-engineer happiness by identifying the variables correlated to melancholy, thereby pinpointing the origins of dysthymia. Or maybe he could bypass melancholy altogether and go right to the source. What is lasting happiness, and how could a dysthymic client find and keep it?

As the obscure head of obfuscation, it was his sole responsibility to display bibliographic exhibits with minimal confusion. To this end, ironically, he relied heavily on assistive technology, for instance, melodious voiceovers in earbuds for holograms of illuminated, handwritten journals; archival images enlarged and projected by microfiche; the sound of riffling flyleaves, jackets, and softcover editions recorded and descriptively narrated in podcasts. The dreamclouds glowed under the rotunda day and night, where the cybrary's visitors could view their welldome analytics before dinner, look up their matchmaking algorithms, or consult a skywalk weather advisory. Caution, denizens. Beware. Of a man and a woman falling out of the sky. It's raining people off the skywalk with a forty percent chance of fatalities. If you witness any falls, text this code. Now the exhibits, graced with paper-fragrance atomizers, are stowed away in the repositories. Did his forgotten handiwork ever make anyone feel a jot of happiness? Bliss? Ecstasy? Joy? Where was the ultimate happiness, after all, in feeling imaginatively transported by carbon symbols on the fibrous pages of an obscure book of genius no one would ever read?

✦

The smog-eating cybrary, unlike stone-and-mortar libraries of yesteryear, harbors no gargoyles, no ivy-dressed pillars, no shelves and no reading nooks, and no security gates behind sliding, bullet-proof plexiglass. It is green. It is not a renovated bank. It does not exchange mazuma, encrypted or not. It is not an analog maker-space. Its green guts are oxygen-generating, always harnessing light, on no occasion static. It is green as nano-sprouted radish and alfalfa, green-breathing in the silent digital lungs of a defunct learning commons. Resembling an observatory, eco-greenhouse, and Christmas tree farm simultaneously, the rotunda of evergreen topiaries once hosted dreamclouds where denizens of the empire downloaded analytics to design micronourishing recipes tailored to their genomes, or streamed the weather on high seas of information, whims of global bonds and securities, waves of cryptocurrency transfers and exchanges, the rise and fall of markets.

Morning, says the mastermind of the happiness machine, who looks like a wolfish, wild-eyed time-traveller out of a trilogy where nomadic tribes of the future immigrate to the moon or leagues under the sea. Morning, says the man a second time, although it is well past noon, when the shadow of Yang's sundial would be shortest in the garden. In a cosmos of unhappy blobs of algal spawn, this man could've set up a biome colony with one or more dystopic elements not dissimilar to ours, i.e. turrets of power and privilege, greed festering in quagmires of bureaucracy, a corrosion of virtue in the name of technological progress. And in this biome, indeed, he sought a cure for dysthymia by reverse-engineering happiness, more or less.

Yang examines the inventor from head to toe, then cautiously offers the gift of dumplings wrapped in a banana leaf.

Morning, says the shaggy mastermind a third time, although it is two minutes past four o'clock *post meridium*. Ignoring the gift, and in a voice bristling with mazuma and pulsing electric currents, the man murmurs: A dreamcloud docking station, it records your negative memories, your trauma, your waking intrusions, flashbacks, and night terrors. Then it adjusts your learned associations with certain subjective phenomena, especially negative recollections. Although subjective, those neurobiological phenomena are measurable and quantifiable. The happiness machine plays them back in the analog cloud of your gray matter with those negative scenarios replaced by good ones.

Our brains are clouds, sir?

In a manner of speaking, yes.

Aren't we more than data fog?

More so than alfalfa, yes.

What does alfalfa have to do with it?

Alfalfa has no gray matter, but we do. That's all. Your alfalfa-insulated pod, withered after the irrigation failed in the mezzopolis, erased from memory forever. A memory of a sibling falling through ice while skating on a frozen lake in winter—the hole in the ice where he drowned—and the subsequent failed rescue efforts would be replaced by no memory of a sibling at all, in other words, one who was never born. Or else, in another variation, be replaced by a new memory of a skating party with a circle of young friends without the sibling, who was never born.

Why not use a happiness planner?

I'd say it's post-positivism.

Why, sir?

The theory itself is not objective, *a posteriori*.

Aren't there other ways to achieve happiness?

This is one, yes.

And if you don't want bad memories adjusted?

You don't want to be happy?

Isn't this escapist, sir?

This dreamcloud adjusts negative traces of past incidents. When I reverse-engineered dysthymia, the algorithms routed me to old-school behavior conditioning. We do have the right to forget, and the right to be forgotten.

Ridiculous, sir.

These traces are neuropsychological phenomena. If you're in a predicament where you started clashing with your significant other the minute you crossed the threshold of your portable pod, you'll recall only the good times in your courtship, maybe a one or two highlights of your honeymoon, and forget the rest.

Isn't this self-deception?

Only an adjustment.

Don't memories constitute our identities?

Well, if you're a depressive type, then making you happy will change your outlook, and hopefully, alter your self-image.

How about serving borscht or seaweed broth to strangers?

I have boxes of kitty grass in my pod right now for my botfree cats, but I'm fresh out of soup. I forgot to exchange my old monographs for food. I believe in the right to forget and the right to be forgotten. When my only daughter died of chronic cyberfatigue syndrome, I felt so overwhelmed, I literally couldn't see my hand in front of my face when I raised it to wash my face in a cloud. The junta commissioned the engineering of a macroviral vaccine for cyberfatigue during the great leap sideways, but it came too late. The great leap sideways was a giant leap backwards. It wasn't about caring for neighbors who lived on both sides of the mezzopolis, or even caring for ourselves—rather, all the denizens of data who disagreed with the junta were excommunicated, then executed in the minefields. You know, I experienced night terrors about her final days. Although her genesis in this world was bioengineered through schizogony—multiple fission, like malaria and other protozoa, not to be confused with nuclear fission—my daughter was one hundred percent human and not at all a bot, yet she was exterminated by the junta in a genocide during the minimization, or as I say, forcefully erased by the muse of herstory. The junta didn't kill her with analog slingshots. Rather, as I said, she was slain by cyberfatigue in the retronym collectives. Forget me, forget-me-not, the junta would hum.

You recall all this trauma?

I wanted to remember, but without triggering panic.

I see, sir.

I'm agoraphobic.

Of course, sir.

Am I panicking now?

Not to my eye, sir.

Are these dumplings? I'm on a diet.

Freeze them if you have an ice box.

Say anything you wish to forget.

Frowning, Yang begins, I recall the last days when the junta destroyed almanacs the gardeners worked so hard to sort, clean up, and index. The angel of translation appeared while I was writing out, in alphanumeric long-hand, a sheaf of receipts by a fireplace, ironically, for the hearthstone tax. I'd prepared a delicious supper of rutabaga cut cross-wise, garnished with mushroom-flavored risotto and truffle-infused olive oil. The angel of translation was cloud-like, a salmon-pink haze of warmth by the hearth, with the melodious voice of a young woman. Guess I'd either worked too hard for the minimization or that the genetically modified oyster mushrooms I used, which tasted like actual oysters, were hallucinogenic. The angel started speaking. *I was born in a quaggy bog of data*, in an alto voiceover with a note of sadness. To this day, I believe she was an apparition of my little datacloud, the private one I built myself and shared with other gardeners, with whom I lost touch after the collapse.

Stop, says the mastermind.

Dreamclouds never worked anyway.

This one did.

All clouds malfunctioned after the collapse.

Don't you have a cloud?

I did but not right now.

Stop mixing happy memories with sad ones.

What if the memories aren't all mine but the angel's? Are my memories of the angel's sad memories also bitter-sweet by proxy? I recall my younger days at the multiver-sity of digerati, and how one morning a beloved systems architect vanished. Later, the autopsy report indicated she'd overdosed on opioids. Diagnosed with comorbid fibromyalgia and dysthymia, going through a spousal estrangement, and her biological daughter away from their pod for the first time as a wisdom warrior in the information wars, she was disillusioned. She grew long brown hair to her waist, no artificial extensions. We used to eat spoonfuls of buttery flan in her statistics seminar, one she'd baked in a bain-marie. A succulent flan concocted of free-range yolks, grassfed goat's milk, and a cream cheese called Saint Angel, which was actually a type of brie. We devoured it in minutes. I wasn't a vegetarian back then. This was long before the shellfish of the disinformation sea were tainted with opioids, thanks to our fentanyl-pickled and propaganda-primed sewage from the data dumps; the mussels, especially, and other filter-feeders like oysters, clams, sea cucumbers. After I turned vegetarian, I didn't miss red meat or fowl, but I do miss seafood. And don't know why Saint Angel was available during the commonwealth's dairy rationing, with the blurry debate about overseas milk quotas.

There you go, hybridizing sadness and happiness.

You ought to design a machine that enhances gratitude instead of a machine that adjusts our memories of trauma. How does self-deception lead to genuine happiness? This is worse than the militia of so-called happiness planners, whose livelihood depended on graphing happiness plots for the dysthymic, how banal. You shouldn't expect your post-traumatic clients to filter their mixed emotions. It's an unrealistic expectation. And your success rate, may I ask?

Don't you have an isolated memory of sadness?

Without our sorrows, we have no counterpoint for

our gratitude. Isn't this a basis for happiness? Or give me joy instead, which is more lasting and less fleeting than happiness.

That's not my definition.

Is there a data standard for happiness, sir?

Look, I don't know you. You showed up on the portal of my pod this morning, or rather, afternoon, and I welcomed you. My advice is, I'd warn you against the use of counterpoint attitudes and emotions, such as gratitude, as footholds for happiness. The junta's wellness propaganda masqueraded as an orthomolecular cure for the tribulations of dysthymic empire and its discontents. We drank a bittersweet tonic of minimization bottled as their museological brand of mystical fascism.

Yang runs his hand along the sleek chrome paneling of the archivist's alfalfa-free pod. Did you ever meet the muse of post-traumatic memory, sir?

Not to my recollection. Did he work with you?

She, sir.

No, don't believe I did.

Do you believe she would've approved of your activities, sir?

Yes, if the junta actually existed.

Why, sir?

The junta fortified the common good.

Do you know that not everybody believes that, sir?

If you think adjusting memories is nonsense, then try this.

Do I have to drink anything, sir?

No, just cut along the dotted lines.

What do you mean, sir?

Cut these statements into strips of paper. Stand on the skykwalk in the evening, read them aloud one by one

to passersby, then press them like stray rose petals or valentines into the hands of strangers. These words will shrink
the radius between love and xenophobia, I promise you.

Are these prayers, blessings?
No.
Valentine candy grams?
None of the above.
Nothing at all?
Just slips of happiness.

. . .

Invisible strawberries are for sale in red seasons.
. . .
Your father and mother do love you, even in war.
. . .
Diaphanous with a glass of red wine, blood—yes.
. . .
Actual word, *dittography*, for repetition in a text.
. . .
God could annihilate us now, start anew—not yet.
. . .
Bitterness and remorse—a bain-marie of humankind.
. . .
Joy stored in your ganglia, a murmur of *aqua vitae*.
. . .
Scarlet velvet rain, a monthly blessing of fertility.
. . .
And don't forget to make flan out of sadness.
. . .

Yang wrinkles his brow in frustration. Frankly, he'd
rather manually clean a minefield of dirty data, or guzzle

a flask of blue-green caffeinated spirulina. With profound disapproval, he scowls at the mastermind of the happiness machine, a stranger with wolfish hair and a voice quavering with yesteryear's ghosts of cryptography. Yang doesn't trust him from one microportal of his pod to the declouded oculus in the rotunda. Why would handing out vapid assertions in the mezzopolis yield happiness in a dysthymic individual who's lost his entire livelihood, thanks to the information wars or the minimization? After the collapse, those flaming females of flamboyant reform vanished without a wiki—not leaving even a wrinkle of their wimples—and no one could gain access to clouds after the apocalypse. Why include this eccentric man as one of the seven harbingers of happiness? Yang remembers. Before embarking on this part of the journey, he completely forgot to daub himself with the immunoglobulin fragrance. He takes the vial out of his dungarees, uncaps the tiny bottle, and holds it under the mastermind's nose.

Wouldn't mind holding one aloft in the twilight if a stranger handed one to me, says the wolfish one, in a friendly voice glowing like watts of halogen light. Yes, then letting go of those slips of happiness fluttering in the night, like will o' wisp in an analog bog. My friend, I'm grieved about the losses incurred by the information wars. Did the muses succeed in minimizing data and revitalizing our creativity? Does figurative language engulf us in falsehoods? Is denotative language an illusion wherein nothing we say actually means what we intend? Are we lying to ourselves? Are metaphors dead? Is a dead metaphor a metaphor? Is a cloud even a cloud? And if a stranger would add a chocolate bonbon with every slippage of language, even more happiness for you, my friend. In other words, if you're ultimately happy

when happiness comes to you, then you're happy. If not,
then not.

     Is dittography a word? asks Yang.

     Look it up in a retronymed lexicon.

     What's the existential purpose in making flan, sir?

     Fill your void with a tasty custard, I guess?

     Sir, what's the marie in a bain-marie, anyway?

     What? It's the bain that matters for a hot bath.

     Wasn't there a Marie whose bath water had healing
qualities, sir?

     Who cares? Seize the day. *Carpe diem*, my friend.

✦

HAPPINESS MACHINE, A SEQUEL

Yes, if only teleological happiness
          existed on slips of paper, namely—
If you are happy
          when happiness comes to you—
please don't fret about what worried us
          making sense of things.

If you are happy,
    then a bit of nonsense on my sleeve
          turns into a flock of birds
crystallizing at the open-air
          bodega on the pier.

If happiness says,
          do not bottle your happiness
to run for fiscal profit on the street—
          enjoy your lemonade without ice,

THE MAZE OF TRANSPARENCIES

liquid smog in summer—
        so acidic, it dissolves tooth enamel,

then in exchange for your anxieties,
            go straight to the welldome
   where the dentist examines you
with a tongue depressor
           made of your delusions.
No cavities, my dear.

At a dreamcloud docked in the waiting room,
you wait
     for a slip of paper.
      It is not a parking validation.

If you are happy
   when happiness comes to you,
     then you are happy.

Ten | The Angel of Translation

THE ANGEL OF TRANSLATION

I wait for the translation angel to show up. Some say
there is no translation angel. Other say she dances at the limits
of figurative language. Some say she satirizes attempts at formal
equivalence. Others say a notion of translation is playing—
in other words, a rogue translation is delinquent,
                              while the good translation is not bad.
The angel of translation says, pay close attention to music
and meaning, not merely syntax. Never wait
for a translation angel
                    to render everything transparent.

‡

By the coordinates decrypted in the black bento box, the
seventh and last harbinger of happiness—with the telos
of a weary pilgrim in search of rejoinders to matters of
the heart—locates Yang by himself in a shanty by the
sea. Why has he looped to the beginning of his own tale?
Yang pauses, lifting his chin into the wind of tall feathergrass. Outside, in a cloudless sky, the sea is afire under
a dropping sun, auburn as glassy coals in a pod-hotel
where his mother and father stayed for a vacation years

ago, coals shiny as root beer candy, as beach bottles rolled and brined by the sea. (The ocean, flanked by its elaborate codices of flora and fauna, unscrolled at a hazy distance— a reserve of beauty and danger where the inky bladders of siphonophores—the little stingmen of war, his father called them—would wash ashore in a posse when a tide of storms churned at the solstice.) At the pod-hotel, he'd pocketed one of the coals, only to be discovered by his father and rebuked sharply; unawares, little Yang had fallen asleep clutching the glass coal in his fist.

Years later, the pod-hotel burned down in one of the mezzopolis's series of turret fires, where one kindling flame led to the deaths of a thousand. Frozen fire, an amber mass of polyresin for an imitation horsehair-bow played by the muse of synthetic music, exploded into the roiling ether, vaporizing the lives of many. (And the sea is not any less beautiful, although it also serves as a blank ledger for the nameless dead, a lexicon without words.) When he was a boy, a ring of fire lay on the other side of the ocean, the motherland of his ancestors who served as warlords, poet-scholars and government officials, barefoot physicans of herbs, and most recently, wisdom warriors for the information wars, and humble gardeners like Yang.

+

To verify the accuracy of his calculations, Yang decodes the black bento box's algorithms nine times—one for each muse of the junta—on his jade abacus. After an hour, Yang takes a deep breath, flexes his shoulders, uncaps the tiny vial, and inhales a whiff of the love-antidote for xenophobia. Momentarily, Yang drifts to the land of analog dreamclouds where polyclonal antibodies eradicate xenophobia in the fiefdoms, even in this cloudfree era of interior monologues on a biosphere gliding on a flotilla of stars as a backdrop to the desolation of Uberasia. (Vaguely, he wonders, aren't we all bots, to an extent? Aren't we all fragments of code, in a way? Isn't deoxyribonucleic acid a script of molecular code? Whose unseen hand wrote our codes in this fleshy program of flora and fauna?) He studies the rough two-dimensional map he plotted before the journey.

Nine times out of nine, the suite of algorithms indubitably points to his seaside shanty, in fact, the precise location where his jade abacus rests on the nightstand. Oddly, this final solution makes no more sense to Yang than adjusting our memories of trauma, or guzzling blue-green chlorophyll. (Or eating a cherry pimiento stuffed in a pickled olive, which he has keenly disliked since boyhood when he was offered one by a classmate and nearly choked.) What does he allegedly know as a harbinger of happiness? Or more precisely, what did the watchful junta observe about Yang's comings and goings that triggered suspicion that he knew something he actually did not? At the final stage of his journey, Yang still has more questions than answers. Or this solution, in essence, presents a *non sequitur.*

Sneezing while he sets a teapot of filtered seawater to boil, Yang ponders the oddness of his pilgrimage. Is happiness reverse-engineerable from disconsolation? And why didn't any of the harbingers of happiness, except the immunological prodigy, seem fundamentally happy? (Because she is a child, I whisper in Yang's ear.) What about the koto musician, the listening artist, or the water doctor? Is it feasible for adults, with the aggregation of mixed blessings, to be completely happy? Do the odds decrease in parts per million of the mezzopolis wherever dysthymia tainted the drinking water? Yang muses aloud. If only an angel of translation could appear and explain this all with transparency and candor. I can't go on repeating these computations. The repetitions verify accuracy but not meaningfulness and validity.

Turning these questions around in his head, Yang sips yerba buena tea infused with bergamot to aid his digestion and reduce flatulence, thanks to bergamot's carminative action. A minute or so into his daydream, Yang realizes he's scribbled on the reverse of his family-tree's cherished recipe for miso soup, which he also keeps on the nightstand, albeit more for sentimental reasons than memory's sake, or rather, the relative ease of proximity. Three tablespoons of homemade fermented miso in boiling water is all. The recipe was translated into an Anglophone tongue for Yang's sake, a 1.5 descendent of immigrants more fluent in Anglophone English than in Mandarin. (Because miso is readily made by fermenting soybeans with salt and *Aspergillus oryzae*—an Uberasian fungus used also for soy sauce and rice vinegar—this recipe calls neither for mass-produced miso, nor freeze-dried wakame seaweed in vacuum-sealed silicone pods.)

+

Simmer water in a small pot
Add 3 T. of miso (see miso recipe)
Add seaweed and cubed tofu (optional)
Garnish with minced green onions
Serve piping hot

+

No grammarian, Yang does wonder—after reading this handwritten translation of a family-tree recipe for the umpteenth time—*why not periods at the ends of the parallel sentences? Punctuation optional,* he decides, I *guess. And how small is a small pot?* Only one quantitative measure is mentioned—three tablespoons. Why not, if it pleased his grandmother to write this way in her arcaded, spider-like hand trained to sketch out the trajectories of space-pods catapulted into outer space where objects designed by humans rarely flew. Yang hummed an imaginary tune in his grandmother's heart as she penned a recipe to her grandson: a verse of memory… half fragrance, half figment? A figment of what, a formula in musical fragments? His grandmother, a grassroots pioneer of data and early sophist of machine learning, wrote in a calligraphic, longhand penmanship, a lost art like the storytelling of silver-haired generations to younger ones, transmitting the wisdom of lived experience through the rise and fall of fortunes through characters, incidents, and leitmotifs in a narrative arc.

As a gardener who computes logarithms and decodes algorithms on a counting frame carved out of a lump of spinach-colored jade, what does he know about storytelling and happiness? Yang speculates. Perhaps the harbingers bring happiness to others, not necessarily themselves. Or it is more about the journey rather than the destination, not about accomplishing this or that? Or is our obsession with happiness, in due course, self-defeating? Yang is unaccustomed to philosophizing outside the customary sandbox of usual ideas. (Is that a dead metaphor, he wonders, wearily.) Did Yang embark on a teleological journey like the Uberasian fable of the stonecutter, the mountain, the cloud, and the sun, a tale which his beaming grandmother would tell him when he was a child, her little peach boy? The stonecutter, who sought to conquer the rough-hewn range whose shadow loomed over his village—the source of his harsh livelihood, and of avalanches, mudslides, and sherpas falling to their precipitous deaths—asked the mountain for wisdom. The mountain said, ask the analog cloud that hides my summit. The cloud, when queried, said, ask the sun that forces me to retreat. The sun said, ask the perilous mountain obstructing my rays. The mountain replied, ask the stonecutter whose mallet and awl chisel at my base, day or night, without mercy. When the stonecutter queried himself, he said aloud—how can it be so that I am the wisest of all? The stonecutter returned to his masonry and asked no more questions.

In his ruminations over tea and a bowl of seaweed broth, Yang believes the logic of this cyclical tale is misleading. The natural elements are neither the stonecutter's coequals nor his inferiors. Rather, the stonecutter is at the mercy of the mountain, the cloud, and the sun. It's not about wisdom, but rather, power. In another version of the tale, a contest might've occurred between the sun and the cloud, both obstructed by the rugged mountain. Or the sun and cloud might compete to display their unique powers—through blazing light or blasting wind—over the stonecutter. What was the telos or ultimate object of the tale? Yang lies awake on his futon meditating on this conundrum long after he's lighted the soy-beeswax votive perfumed with the fragrance of black cherries and wisteria, and forgotten to snuff it out.

And what about the lovely tale of a peach boy his grandmother would recount, time after time, with delightful nods of her silvering head? On a foggy bank of dreamclouds, Yang drifts to the blossoming orchard where his grandmother, seating him upon her lap, would enthrall him with the tale of a baby boy who, buoyed inside a giant peach, floated down a river into a childless, elderly couple's arms. When he was of age, he'd vanquish the ogres, wolves, and bandits attacking the village. The peach boy's adoptive parents—the elderly couple—would pack a bento box of mochi that Yang loved as a child, those hand-pounded glutinous rice cakes. Even now, Yang's childhood memory eludes the dream or vice versa—did vicious wolves attack the village in this recollected version of the tale? Was the peach orchard not a utopia, after all? Did his silver-haired grandmother mention ogres or bandits? Was it all of the above or none?

What is it that we truly know about happiness? Yang tosses on his futon. The question, like a geometric rose, spirals outward on its velveteen core. Does happiness reside in the eye of the beholder? Does it live in the beclouded hearts of those who generate it, mine it, or those who ingest and use it? Like data, is happiness possessed by those who analyze its symmetries, its finite warp and weft like an infinite tapestry, or is it possessed by those who consume it—for instance, denizens who architect and analyze data for the common good—to decrease hunger and increase wages when salaries existed, to put loaves of rosemary olive oil bread in kitchen pods and indigo textiles in weaver's looms? Is happiness obtained by vanquishing xenophobia? How could we have survived an era of connectivity and cloudsourced data yet still emerge plagued by xenophobia? What about the analyst whose endless shoals of grief over her young son nearly brought her to mercies of the angel of the future, the man on the skywalk who saved the oppressed from leaping to their deaths? Did the museological

junta believe that happiness and sorrow mingled in coex-
istence to draw our attention to joy of a profounder, san-
guine kind than transitory happiness?

I mutter in Yang's ear, but I don't think he can hear
me. You call me the angel of translation, for what is a cloud
but an angel with shot-off wings? Actually, I am your
rogue translator, my dear sleeping gardener, one whose
fragmentary scripts and validations and translations, re-
phrased within this lexical lattice, communicate only a
slice of this diced cosmos. What I've translated for you all
these years, even now, when you can only hear me in your
post-apocalyptic dreams, when the lightrail no longer runs
by the minute or even the hour, and a smog-eating cybrary
sags under the burden of globalization compacted into lost
clouds, not books—when melancholy and trauma cannot
be erased because not even a mastermind singled out by
the muse of post-traumatic memory can isolate sad ones
from happy ones, I am still utterly transparent to you.
Dear post-datum gardener, if you only knew. This angelic
transparency renders me invisible by nature. You can no
longer communicate with me. In their zeal to control the
expansion of knowledge and revitalize, nay, to resuscitate
the creative imagination—the muses of postmodern herstory, synthetic music, astrophysics or radioastronomy,
love and comedy in stereo as romantic comedy, epic poetry slam, electrochoreography, post-traumatic memory,
and domestic tragedy—none of the nine members of the
junta granted you amnesty to access the cloudsourced data
you once loved. Haunted by an ostensible angel of translation—a rogue interpreter of tongues and pseudomuse of
interlingual renditions—do you harbor a solitary crumb
of happiness on this earthbound journey of hybridized
bliss and blight?

Yang has fallen asleep, his votive still alight. Snoring gently, he dreams of falling inside a vertical, lightless elevator shaft, and it occurs to Yang, even while dreaming, that our lifecycles and biomass, perchance, operate as thought experiments designed in a protean, ever-changing workspace of genesis—the alpha and omega, not always predictable in a quantum universe of nonlocality. Not in our strategic mitigation of drought, biofuel shortages, and famine, or in our use of predictive analytics to quash odious ills like xenophobia—so ingrained, the designs of war and hate are inscribed in our chromosomes—have we found that mining big data yields joy. (It does not, dear reader.) By doing so, we limit an unquantifiable degree of happiness, unforetold by fizzling electrons of the universe in fleeting states of excitation. (What, for instance, is the happiness of an atom, and the pleasures of a proton? Or the ecstasy of an electron?)

The votive burns brightly as a celestial body while Yang sleeps.

Yang dreams of his boyhood in superblooming meadows, acres of marigolds and black-eyed susans under low-swept skies, when he'd run back home with excitement after his mathematics tutor invited him to the front of a classroom to solve trigonometry equations with the fat chalk said to mark railroad ties before the magnetic light-rails. His mother waited with a tray of almond cookies and tea or milk, and his father would return early, if it were a Friday, from the actuarial datamines, which he'd facetiously dubbed his fact-finding fortress of data forensics, unwittingly calling out the future for his gangly-legged son, the math whiz who asked for glasses at nine years old because his favorite tutor wore them, not because he was myopic. As a young man, Yang longed to understand more than what cardinal numbers told him, in other words, how they spelled out an exquisite sequence of stories that, if assembled in a bog of gigadata, could improve the lives of those around him. However, its idealogues ascended to power, a paranoid mindset doubled by a nagging temptation of self-preservation inevitably took root and flowered, causing dogmatism and despotism to masquerade hand-in-hand, miserably.

The wick sputters but the flame does not go out.

You know the end of this story, dear reader. With the minimization yet to fade from post-traumatic memory although its muse has vanished, and without the assistance of a functioning happiness machine, and the question of whether an immunoglobulin fragrance can eradicate xenophobia, you survive as one of the stewards of what the muses gleaned from their qualitative and quantitative search for a common good by controlling data surfeit, ultimately distilled to a précis of love, and of course, loving one another.

I whisper into Yang's ear. Take good care of what is entrusted to you. *Do all the good you can. By all the means you can. In all the ways you can. In all the places you can. At all the times you can. To all the people you can. As long as you ever can.* You only have this earthbound journey, a system of maddeningly byzantine intricacies. Your soul is anchored by a miasma of quantum bits and megabytes, your only chance to engage in the design of the alpha and omega. You will never return. After this life, the rose-colored wheel of breath does not spin again. *It will happen in a moment, in the blink of an eye, when the last trumpet is blown. For when the trumpet sounds, those who have died will be raised to live forever. And we who are living will also be transformed.*

Subliminally, does Yang remember how to pray, even in sleep? His mother used to pray for him while he slept, didn't she? Not memorized prayers, except for one she referred to as a doxology, and one she described as a common prayer—in a spirit of heavenly jazz, she improvised her prayers—first, in the classical Mandarin tongue of Uberasia, succeeded by a tongue known to no one except the alpha and omega, the heavenly tongue of angels, she used to say, as well. Into his auditory subconscious flowed her mysterious utterances, those glossariums sung while, as a boy, he breathed until his eyelids fluttered and his mother's egg-shaped chin arose and—with a teacup nightlight on the wall—he left an aromatic cloud of orange blossom and clove oil called happiness, unbeknownst to little Yang, whose boyish limbic system and juvenile visual cortex had already drifted to a realm of superblooming meadows and buzzing seven-year cicadas, where starry nubs of railroad chalk dotted a night sky with needle-eye constellations unstitched from the textiles of ancient lore. Who was the flying horse, and why did this horse sprout wings? The proud queen who bragged about her beauty, unequalled by sea nymphs, who was exiled to swivel around the north star? The eagle who clutched thunderbolts? Were Yang's parents and grandparents, some who perished in the great-great wars, translated into celestial bodies in the heavens?

Deep sky objects, no more.

A fragrance of black cherries and wisteria fills the room with clouds of liquid nitrogen or cotton candy, the spun floss of flavored sugar. Yang soars in a dreamcloud which he has diligently cultivated over the duration of his years, sharing it with other gardeners. He does not realize those for whom we tilled the earth without reward, for love's own sake, may never fully grasp the clay geologies of their blemished loves, the ones for whom our sacrifice is most worthy. (Perishable data, whose values decrease with time.) Ashy petals of breath fill the biosphere for a moment, the faceless nine muses of the junta, for whom Yang toiled because he believed in museological virtues of a meaningfully informed minimization, sabotaged their ubiquitous dogma—a far cry from a flower-wielding utopia, the right to be forgotten in the fiefdoms. Was it all for naught?

Verba volant, scripta manent. Words fly away, yet writings remain.

With much of the world's flotsam and jetsam absorbed into clouds of information—amorphous datamines and lexical glossariums—those syllabaries of knowledge weigh on Yang's heart, the figurative coordinates where his body and soul, invisible and visible, hover in an immaterial sandwich of dirt and sky. Throughout his years, he has met denizens who've obtained a second chance after receiving bioprosthetic valves, hydrogel corneas, or ovoid polyurethane hearts. (In the winter of their lives, granted an opportunity or second chance, grace refreshed their vitality.) Asleep, Yang's four-chambered, bicameral heart—with its wings and auricles of expanded knowledge—shines like a hygroscopic salt rock hewn out of an Uberasian mountain quaking on other side of the world, where the alpha and omega dwells in unapproachable light. The obscure saint of artificial intelligence glows like a jug of citronella oil ignited by a spark, as a midsummer swarm of honeybees kissed by lightning in an electric storm, as martyrs burned alive—torches lighting a nocturnal colosseum in a dying empire before the common era.

Do not wait for the translation angel to render everything transparent.

EPILOGUE

THE TRANSLATION ANGEL SPEAKS

I shall greet you at last, my love, in your mother tongue
as I mingle in lexical spaces with diacritics, acute or grave—
a mystical triptych of integrity, an ethos of labor,
and lavish grace from above.
        Do not wait for me, dear reader,
                in this maze of transparencies.
And if you're asked who said so,
                an answer might be, a cloud did.
Yes, let's just say a cloud wrote
        this little chronicle of happiness.

✦ ✦ ✦

ACKNOWLEDGEMENTS

In a slightly altered form, portions of this novel have appeared in *The Collagist, Diode, The Ellis Review*, and *Moria*. Special thanks to Nicole Borello, Matt Bell, Jasmine Cui, Linda Dove, Logan February, Matthew Olzmann, and Patty Paine for giving a home to those nascent visions over the years, and especially to Eugene Lim and Joanna Sondheim for their generosity and grace; Jeremy Hoevenaar for very astute proofreading; and Corey Frost for his exquisite cover design. I also express my gratitude to wonderful colleagues at Point Loma Nazarene University, who befriended the flowering of this poetic imagination.

✦ ✦ ✦

END NOTES

CHAPTER ONE

The noosphere is a term used by Pierre Teilhard de Chardin (1881-1955), a French philosopher and Jesuit priest, in his 1925 essay, "L'hominisation." It refers to a conceptual sphere of human consciousness that influences the biosphere.

The dirigibles like artificial moons lighting up the night sky are inspired by illumination satellites at the Xichang Satellite Launch Center. The organization responsible for the project is the Tian Fu New Area Science Society, led by Wu Chunfeng. Read more in *The Indian Express*, "China to launch artificial moon to light up night sky."

The phrase, "garbage in, garbage out," (a.k.a. GIGO) is an idiom for saying that "input is no better than output." *Urban Dictionary*. 27 February 2014.

The quality of drinking water, clean mountain air, frequent dentist visits, and bikeability are traits of the happiest cities in the United States. The role of a "happiness planner" is briefly described as well. "These are the happiest cities in the United States" by Dan Buettner. *National Geographic*. 18 October 2017.

"...more blessed it is to give than receive." Acts 20:35, *New International Version*.

The information about jellyfish blooms and global oscillation is available from the NAS. Robert H. Condon, Carlos M. Duarte, Kylie A. Pitt, et al. "Recurrent jellyfish blooms are a consequence of global oscillations." Proceedings of the National Academy of Sciences. January 2013; 110 (3): 1000-1005. DOI: 10.1073/pnas.1210920110.

Supertasters and their demographics. Antonietta Robino, Massimo Mezzavilla, Nicola Pirastu, Maddalena Dognini, Beverly J. Tepper, Paolo Gasparini. "A Population-Based Approach to Study the Impact of PROP Perception on Food Liking in Populations along the Silk Road." PLoS One. 2014; 9(3): e91716. 2014 Mar 13. DOI: 10.1371/journal.pone.0091716

CHAPTER TWO

The logic puzzle, "Circular Amphitheater," is paraphrased from Logicville, a site maintained by Martin Gardener. Accessed 28 May 2018.

Slow light refers to a discovery by scientists at the University of Glasgow. "Scientists slow down the speed of light traveling in free space." 23 January 2015. *Science Daily*.

THE MAZE OF TRANSPARENCIES

CHAPTER THREE

The story of the reclusive Russian mathematician refers to Grigori Perelman: "If the proof is correct, no other recognition is needed." Read more about Perelman in "Manifold Destiny: A legendary problem and the battle over who solved it" by Sylvia Nasar and David Gruber. *The New Yorker*. 28 August 2006.

CHAPTER FOUR

The story of the angel on the skywalk is a fiction inspired by Chen Si, known as the Angel of Nanjing, China. "Hero has stopped over 300 people from throwing themselves off the Nanjing bridge in the last 13 years." *The Shanghaiist*. 23 August 2016.

CHAPTER FIVE

The story of the rainfall bowl is a fiction inspired by Ayyappa Masagi, who is known as India's "water doctor." *Your Story: Think Change India*. Accessed 28 May 2018.

John Dalberg-Action (1834-1902) is the baron who says, "Absolute power corrupts absolutely," and "History is a not a web woven by innocent hands."

CHAPTER SIX

The four genes linked to longevity are described in this article. "Living to 100: New Genes for Longevity Found" by Rachael Rettner. *Live Science*. 18 December 2015.

"Dysfunction eats strategy for brunch" is a variation on a quotation often attributed to Peter Drucker, who said, "Culture eats strategy for breakfast."

The phrase, *finite longing for the infinite,* is an allusion to Emmanuel Levinas on metaphysical desire and Friedrich Schlegel.

"The heart has its reasons of which reason knows nothing" is credited to Blaise Pascal.

CHAPTER SEVEN

The phrase, *bread and circus*, is attributed to the poet Juvenal in first century Rome.

The Japanese word *karoshi* refers specifically to death from overwork. "Japanese Has a Word for 'Working to Death'" by Jake Edelstein and Mari Yamamoto. *The Daily Beast*. 3 February 2017.

Love is as strong as death is paraphrased from Song of Songs 6:8, *New International Version*: "Place me like a seal over your heart, like a seal on your arm; for love is as strong as death, its jealousy unyielding as the grave. It burns like blazing fire, like a mighty flame."

CHAPTER EIGHT

The average brain has a hundred billion neurons, which is approximately the same number of stars in the Milky Way. "Why Your Brain Is Like the Universe." *BrainMD Health*. Accessed 19 August 2018.

CHAPTER NINE

The smog-eating library is loosely based on a building in Taipei designed by the Belgian architect, Vincet Callebaut. Juvina Lai. "Smog-eating tower featuring luxury apartments in Taipei opening soon." *Taiwan News*. 4 August 2017.

Opioids in shellfish are reported in Puget Sound, Seattle. "Traces of Opioids Found in Seattle-Area Mussels" by Vanessa Romo. *National Public Radio* (NPR). 25 May 2018.

The phrases on slips of paper ("slips of happiness") are quoted from my chapbook, *What the Sea Earns for a Living*. San Mateo, California: Quaci Press 2014.

CHAPTER TEN

The following phrases are attributed to John Wesley: *Do all the good you can. By all the means you can. In all the ways you can. In all the places you can. At all the times you can. To all the people you can. As long as you ever can.*

1 Corinthians 15:52, *New Living Translation: It will happen in a moment, in the blink of an eye, when the last trumpet is blown. For when the trumpet sounds, those who have died will be raised to live forever. And we who are living will also be transformed.*

SOURCES CONSULTED

Gleick, James. *The Information: A History, A Theory, A Flood.* New York: Vintage 2012.

"Glossary of Key Information Security Terms, National Institute of Standards and Technology (NIST)." Accessed 1 November 2017. http://nvlpubs.nist.gov/nistpubs/ir/2013/NIST.IR.7298r2.pdf

"European Union: Language and Terminology." Accessed 2 December 2017. https://ec.europa.eu/agriculture/glossary_en

Hansen, Joel. "Standard Mandarin: Chinese Pronunciation." Accessed 20 May 2018. Copenhagen, Denmark. http://www.standardmandarin.com/

Hu, Tung-Hui. *A Prehistory of the Cloud.* Boston, Massachusetts: MIT Press 2016.

@latinphr. Latin phrases in original and translation. *Twitter.* 2018.

"National Initiative for Cybersecurity Careers and Studies." U.S. Department of Commerce. National Institute of Standards and Technology. Accessed 1 November 2017. https://niccs.us-cert.gov/glossary

"Preparing for the General Data Protection Regulation (GDPR): 12 steps to take now." Information Commissioner's Office, European Union. Accessed 20 November 2017. https://ico.org.uk/media/1624219/preparing-for-the-gdpr-12-steps.pdf

✦ ✦ ✦

KAREN AN-HWEI LEE is the author of three poetry collections, *Phyla of Joy* (Tupelo 2012), *Ardor* (Tupelo 2008) and *In Medias Res* (Sarabande 2004). Her book of literary criticism, *Anglophone Literatures in the Asian Diaspora: Literary Transnationalism and Translingual Migrations* (Cambria 2013), was selected for the Cambria Sinophone World Series. She also authored a novel, *Sonata in K* (Ellipsis 2017), and translated a volume of Li Qingzhao's collected poetry and prose, *Doubled Radiance* (Singing Bone 2018). The recipient of a National Endowment for the Arts Grant, Lee lives in San Diego and serves in the administration at Point Loma Nazarene University.

ellipsis
• • •
press